SUDDEN SMOKE

"I say you're a sneaking dark-o'-the-moon cow thief, Kid," Jake Kelhorn snapped. "I say that you could tell where every cow that's been missing from the Winged-H these last few weeks has gone to. I say it to your face, and I'm asking what you're going to do about it!"

"This!" the Rimrock Kid shouted, and his hand fell toward his holster.

That was when Rowdy Dow jumped. Not toward the Kid, nor toward Kelhorn and the others at the bar, but toward the table where two more Winged-H hands were already reaching for guns. Their guns were half out of holsters when the edge of the table caught them across their chests and sent them bowling over backward, their chairs splintering beneath them. The saloon had become a thundering inferno of roaring guns.

"Get out of here, Kid!" Rowdy shouted. *"They've stacked the odds!"*

The Kid shot one hasty, grateful glance toward Rowdy and was gone through the batwings. . . .

The Devil's Saddle

NORMAN A. FOX

A DELL BOOK

Published by
Dell Publishing
a division of
Bantam Doubleday Dell Publishing Group, Inc.
1540 Broadway
New York, New York 10036

The characters, places, incidents, and situations in this book are
imaginary and have no relationship to any person, place, or actual
happening.

ISBN: 0-440-21056-9

Printed in the United States of America

Published simultaneously in Canada

August 1994

10 9 8 7 6 5 4 3 2 1

FOR RICHARD

1

HOODED HORSEMEN

The letter which was to fetch Rowdy Dow and Stumpy Grampis toward the forgotten town of Dryfooting was a mixture of urgency, illiteracy, and ink blots. That it had managed to reach them that winter was itself a tribute to the efficiency of the mails and enough to make a postmaster-general do a bit of preening, for that pair of trouble-shooting partners had holed-up in a cabin in the Little Belts, resolved to roundside in comfort and let 'er snow. Then the letter had arrived. To Rowdy Dow, puzzling over it by lamplight for the 'steenth time, while Stumpy waited, with no great show of patience, at a ready checkerboard, the letter held mystery and allure and the possibilities of profit. Also, there was a hint of danger. To Rowdy, of whom a weird likeness had until recently adorned many a reward dodger, the stillness of snowy hills had become stagnation. He was an ex-outlaw, but a governor's pardon hadn't necessarily turned him into a petrified man. Here was a chance to stretch his legs.

The letter, addressed to Rowdy, had said: "I've got a proposition for a man of your caliber, and I'd like to talk it over with you. Reckon you've heard tell of Griffen's Gold. I can cut you in on a share of it, if you've got half the brains your rep gives you credit for. If you're interested, come to Dryfooting and put up at the Seraglio House. Say nothing to nobody, and I'll get in touch with you as soon as I hear you're in town. Watch yourself."

To this cryptic message had been appended the warped signature of one Caleb Hackett.

Stumpy, who had unblushingly read the missive over

Rowdy's shoulder the day the letter had come, frowned his bewilderment. "What in tarnation is Griffen's Gold?" he demanded.

"Dunno," Rowdy said reflectively. "Seems I've heard of it before, though. A buried treasure, the back of my head tells me. Maybe we should go into business, old hoss. 'You lose it—we'll find it,' will be our slogan."

"This here letter don't say nothing about me," Stumpy observed with stiff dignity.

"Hackett's probably heard about you and figures you can't read anyway," Rowdy offered as a solace.

Whereupon the subject of the letter had been dropped. Rowdy had stuffed the missive into a pocket of his pearl-buttoned shirt, and, although his re-reading of it became a ritual in the days that followed, nothing more was said. Until this night. That letter had become as omnipresent as a belled sheep at a cattlemen's picnic. It had swelled until it thrust at the walls of the cabin; it had whispered at the keyhole and yowled under the eaves; it had taken all the fun out of roundsiding. The Serpent, stamped and postmarked, had crept into Eden. And that was why Stumpy, contemplating the checkerboard, was likewise contemplating surrender to the inevitable. But not with grace.

"How far away do you reckon Dryfooting is?" he asked sourly.

"It's in the badlands country along the Missouri," Rowdy said dreamily.

Stumpy sighed. He'd looked forward to at least another thirty days of the solid comfort this cabin provided; he'd anticipated thirty more evenings with the checkerboard and the ancient mail-order catalog which comprised the cabin's library. Aye, that was the rub, leaving the catalog behind. Confound Rowdy Dow for an itch-heeled galoot who didn't know when he was well off! Stumpy shoved the checkerboard aside and reached for the catalog.

Give a man a mail-order catalog for company and you have given him the world. Here is the perfect impetus to day-dreaming. If his longing is for literature, there is always a gaudy book section. If music be his meat and drink, there are guitars to be picked—from the index. Should he pine for the saddle he will someday buy, he can put in innumerable hours selecting one, and he can even write up the order—not forgetting to state size and color —and set the whole thing aside, pending a day when his finances are less feeble. If a chicken farm is the rainbow of his seeking, there are pages devoted to egg baskets and flock feeders and various vile potions designed to kill lice and mites. And should it be feminine companionship he craves, there is no dearth of pulchritude to be examined. Aye, the universe lies between those colored covers!

"I won't do it!" Stumpy said firmly. "You can moon around all you want, Rowdy, staring at me like Gawd's own conscience, but I ain't budging from here. Not for all the gold in Montana. Do I make myself clear?"

"Sure," said Rowdy. "Let's forget the whole thing."

And that is how it came about that a fortnight later found these two riding stirrup to stirrup through a land that looked like it had been left over from the making of the world, a land of pagan beauty and awesome grandeur, sinister and fantastic and lonely—the badlands of the Missouri. Nature had used a lavish brush here; buttes were barred with horizontal stripes of all the rainbow's hues, and the sage was silvered, and dark cedars grew on eroded slopes. Nature had been wantonly prodigious with her chisel, too; sandstone had been shaped by wind and weather into semblances of medieval castles and porticoed mansions and unearthly monsters and things quite mad. It was a land serene and incredible, breath-taking and eternal.

Spring had come early here; the stillness of a snowy sanctuary in the Little Belts seemed like something belonging to a remote past. Wild flowers—primroses, prickly pear, and chokecherry blossoms—were beginning to show themselves; the breeze was like a warm caress; a dead land was stirring to life. But to all this Stumpy Grampis turned a jaundiced eye. Even when their trail took them out upon a rocky escarpment with a wide panorama sweeping away below them, Stumpy refused to show enthusiasm as they sat their saddles and viewed the breath-taking vista.

"Bet this Caleb Hackett will turn out to be loonier than a hooty owl," Stumpy prophesied. "If the galoot's got hidden gold, why's he wantin' to share it? Had an uncle once that behaved the same way. Allus lookin' for lost mines, he was. Mailed letters to anybody that might be interested. Finally he cracked up for sure. Tied a tag on his wrist, addressin' hisself to the Lost Dutchman Mine, stuck postage stamps all over his forehead, and tried to climb into a mail sack. Figgered he'd mail hisself to the lost mine. Do you know what he's doin' right now?"

"Looking at mail-order catalogs?" Rowdy suggested.

Stumpy snorted and fell silent.

They made an incongruous pair as they rested here. Rowdy, according to obsolete reward dodgers, was five foot eleven, weighed one hundred and seventy pounds, and had a mop of black hair, inclined to curl. Some might have called him handsome, but his was a choir boy's face, cherubic and disarming. He was twenty-eight years old, while Stumpy, if the truth were known, was twice that age, a little man, leathery and grizzled, with a sprinkling of frost in his thinning hair and down-tilted mustache. Chance had made partners of them; some sort of illogical attraction of opposites kept them together. Both wore range garb, but Rowdy's clothes included bench-made boots, foxed trousers, and a certain amount of fooforaw in the trimmings. Stumpy's garb looked as if he slept in it—which he often did. Yet in many ways they were two of a kind; both had heard the owl hoot, as the saying went, and dangers they'd shared had made them kin. Rowdy, shaping up a cigarette now, instinctively passed the makings to Stumpy.

"Sounds like a stagecoach coming," Rowdy opined. "And hell for leather, too. Darned if I wasn't beginning to feel like we were the only people left in the world."

"I make 'er out now," Stumpy said, his eyes probing the distance. "You ever see a coach like that one?"

They had balcony seats in an amphitheater, and, across the vast openness stretching below them, a road snaked from north to south, winding in and out among the clustering boulders and misshapen monoliths studding the floor. Along that road came a coach, its six horses lashed to a wild gallop. But it was not the evidence of frantic flight that interested the partners, but the coach itself.

The vehicle drawing nearer, they could see that it was in some respects a conventional enough Concord, its stout body, slung upon leather thoroughbraces, a tribute to New England craftsmanship. Its arching roof had the usual railing around the outer edge; and luggage was piled high here. There was a front boot and a rear boot, the latter covered by a leather curtain. It was the color of the coach that had startled Stumpy. Blue and red and green made the body something to catch the eye; the wheels were a blur of gold. The spokes had been gilded. The horses appeared to have high, waving plumes upon their collars; and Rowdy, whose eyes were better than his partner's, would have sworn that the lines were silver.

But now Rowdy had seen what was giving this coach such frantic impetus, and his interest shifted. Perhaps a quarter of a mile behind the Concord, a half-dozen horsemen had swung into view—horsemen wearing pointed hoods of sorts, made, Rowdy judged, of flour sacks with eye-holes cut into them. These masked riders were hell-bent upon overtaking the coach. Rowdy could hear the popping of guns now, and see the tiny spurts of smoke from six-shooters in the pursuers' hands.

Each minute was bringing the coach nearer, though always it was below the partners. Rowdy could see that two people were upon its high seat, a youngish man or woman who handled the ribbons and plied the whip, and an older man, his white beard whipping in the wind, who clung beside the driver. Rowdy, wishing for field glasses, decided that no one was inside the coach. Its interior seemed to be piled high with luggage. And then, while the pair watched in breathless silence, disaster overtook the coach.

A small boulder in the road was the Concord's undoing. A front wheel struck this boulder; the coach seemed to leap into the air, and then the vehicle, the wheel shattered, was tilting crazily and dragging upon the axle. Dust billowed upward; the horses came to a rearing stop, anchored by that dragging axle, and the man and the girl spilled to the ground. No doubt now about her being a girl. Buckskin garbed her, a short, fringed skirt and a jacket to match; while her aged companion wore black broadcloth. The two went darting toward a group of boulders to the far side of the coach, but the girl had taken time to wrench a rifle from the front boot and was toting it with her.

"Damn!" Stumpy breathed and got his six-shooter out of leather.

"Too far away," Rowdy judged and laid a restraining hand upon his partner's arm. "You reckon we could find a switchback leading down to the floor?"

Stumpy, scanning the rocky slope stretched below

them at a dangerous tilt, muttered something about mountain goats. Those hooded horsemen were almost upon the abandoned coach. The six had fanned out wide; the girl's rifle was speaking from the boulders which she and her companion had gained, and suddenly Rowdy was watching with rapt attention. That girl could shoot! She was tossing lead with an efficiency that sent the pursuit turning tail. Masked men spilled off horses and took to the nearest cover with alacrity that showed a sudden respect for the girl's rifle. But, hunkered down among the rocks, they returned the girl's fire, and the tableau below was thus turned into a siege.

"The odds are pretty heavy," Rowdy remarked. "Let's find a trail, old hoss, and buy in."

"Looks like somebody else has bought in," Stumpy observed.

And it was true. Across the rocky amphitheater, another rifle was speaking from the far slope. His eyes keening the distance, Rowdy made out the minute figure of a man and glimpsed a checkered shirt as the fellow began carefully moving down the slope, scuttling from cover to cover. Rowdy's brow pleated. Checkered Shirt was aiming at the masked men, firing over the heads of the girl and her aged companion, and that made him an ally of the besieged pair. But what had placed Checkered Shirt here at this opportune time? Had he been pacing the fancy stagecoach on the far slope, anticipating this attack? Or was he some wayfarer like Rowdy and Stumpy who'd seen the siege and decided to take cards?

Rowdy shook his head, his attention again drawn elsewhere. One of those hooded men had deserted the rock that sheltered him and was bellying across the ground, propelling himself by his elbows and knees and keeping as low as possible. The fellow had chosen a commendable strategy; he was circling so that the abandoned stagecoach

was always between himself and the man and the girl in
the rocks on its far side. Thus he was not menaced by the
girl's remarkable rifle. And his friends were seeing that
the girl stayed holed-up while this lone marauder made
his play.

Nearer the coach, the fellow came to his hands and
knees and made better progress, scuttling across the open
ground like a gigantic crab. His real menace now was
from the rifle in Checkered Shirt's hands, but the closer
the hooded man came to the coach, the less was his danger. Checkered Shirt was too far down the slope to see
him now. Suddenly the hooded man came to a stand,
dashed to the coach and began tugging at some object
that was lashed to the tilted top, just inside the railing.

Rowdy got his six-shooter out, laid it across his left
forearm, sighted carefully, then put the gun away. The
distance was still too great for a revolver, and he wished
mightily that he and Stumpy had seen fit to fetch a rifle
along. Watching, he saw the hooded man free the object
he was after, then turn and dart clumsily away with it. His
prize was burlap-wrapped, but something about its shape
gave Rowdy the clue. "A saddle!" he said in vast astonishment. "The galoot risked his hide for a saddle!"

The man with the saddle was running as hard as he
could, burdened as he was, but he was still keeping the
coach between himself and the girl. Now he caught up
the reins of a horse that had been left standing when the
masked men had taken to the rocks. Still clutching the
saddle, he got astride the horse and brought the mount
around and prodded it to a run, taking a zig-zag course
away from the coach and directly toward the slope upon
which Rowdy and Stumpy perched. There was a moment
when Rowdy could have caught him in his sights, and,
since the man was drawing nearer, ever nearer, perhaps
the distance wouldn't have been too great. But that mo-

ment was lost when the hooded horseman and the stolen saddle disappeared under an overhang below.

The girl had now discovered the theft. She was peppering bullets after the horseman, but the coach was in her way, and obviously she didn't dare maneuver for a better position. Not with those other hooded men keeping her penned by intermittent shooting. Checkered Shirt, Rowdy discovered, had worked down to the bottom of the far slope and was attempting to get closer to the girl. But now those hooded gunmen were making a wild break for the horses they'd so hastily deserted. All five of them made it into saddles and turned north again; the girl was still concentrating on the sixth man, and that gave the others their chance. And it was that sixth horseman who concerned Rowdy.

"Listen!" he cried. "Hear those rocks clattering? There *is* a switchback up this slope. Our friend is climbing it. Stumpy, here's where we buy in. Me, I crave to know just what makes a kak so valuable that six men risk their hides for it."

The partners began moving along the rimrock, leading their horses, and Rowdy cast another glance below. The five were making dust in the distance; the girl had come out of the rocks and was standing spread-legged, her rifle up and blazing to speed the five on their way. This indicated that the sixth man had managed to lose himself to her view on the slope. Checkered Shirt was on the rim now, coming to join the girl. If the whole point of this attack had been to get the saddle, the marauders had succeeded; for the three below had no mounts with which to make a pursuit. The work done, the other five raiders were withdrawing, satisfied, apparently, that the one who'd stolen the saddle would gain the rimrock and safety. And that one was almost to the top of the ascent; Rowdy could hear the labored breathing of the horse.

And Rowdy had found the trail which led up here. It wound between two shoulder-high boulders, and Rowdy, dropping the reins of his horse and ground-anchoring it among sheltering rocks, lifted a lariat from the saddle. Uncoiling the rope, he passed an end to Stumpy, crossed the trail and stationed himself in the shadow of the farthest boulder. Stumpy wordlessly hunkered down by the opposite boulder, the rope lying between them on the trail; and they were this way when the hooded horseman hove into view.

What happened then happened so quickly that it was hard to have any coherent understanding of it afterward. The timing of the two was good enough; one instant they glimpsed the hooded man bearing down the trail, the next the two had leaped to a stand and were hoisting the rope and drawing it taut. By all that was natural, the hooded rider should have caromed into that rope and been spilled from the saddle; but perhaps he saw the rope in the last split second. The fellow's right hand was holding the reins; under his left arm he awkwardly carried the burlap-wrapped saddle. Instinctively he threw up his left arm to protect his face; the saddle spilled to the ground just as the man fed steel to his mount, throwing the horse against the rope.

He was so close to Rowdy at that moment that Rowdy might have reached out and touched him. Rowdy saw the man's sinewy leg, Levi-clad, saw his worn boot and a spur that had suddenly turned red. He even saw that some of the tines were missing from the rowel. Then the rope was burning through Rowdy's hands as the horse lunged hard against it; and horse and rider were past Rowdy and streaking down the trail.

Branding himself several varieties of fool for not having waited gun in hand, Rowdy reached for his gun now. His fancy trick had proved an utter failure; that's what a man got for trying to be theatrical. But again Rowdy was frustrated. The hooded horseman had lost himself around a turn of the trail; he bobbed into view once again, farther away, and then was gone from sight.

"That," said Rowdy with disgust, "just goes to show that if you live right and are kind to old ladies and lost dogs, luck will always side with you."

"Leastwise we got the kak," Stumpy observed.

Rowdy picked up the burlap-wrapped saddle and with it in his arms, strode back to the edge of the rimrock. Down below he could see the girl and the man in the checkered shirt charging across the open space between the stagecoach and the near slope as though determined to take up the pursuit on foot. Rowdy, skylined, shouted, "Here's your saddle—!"

He intended to add that he'd be down with it shortly, but he never got to that. The girl took one look, recognized the saddle, lifted her rifle, and Rowdy felt his sombrero being wrenched away. The rifle spoke a second time, and Rowdy was minus a lock of hair before he had sense enough to fall backward out of the line of that devastating rifle.

"Danged if this ain't your unlucky day," Stumpy observed with scant sympathy. "All that girl seems to have in her head is that anybody who's got her kak must be on the wrong side of the fence. What you going to do now?"

"Pack this saddle to Dryfooting and turn it over to the law," Rowdy growled. "If she wants it, she can get it from the sheriff. Me, I'm through trying to play Good Samaritan for that lady. Look at my J.B.! Forty dollars' worth of hat shot to hell'n gone. Come on, Stumpy, before she climbs up the slope and lets daylight through us. We're getting out of here."

2

Dryfooting, that scabrous growth on the badlands' beauty, had warred with the weather for twenty years and lost every battle. Winds had peeled the paint from the rickety row of false-fronts that comprised the main street; snows had burdened ridgepoles until the buildings had gotten a sway-backed look to them. Dryfooting was a cowtown, and, in the opinion of transient drummers, the cows were welcome to it. This sad collection of habitations had gotten its name from a dusty tributary of the Missouri, a meandering and altogether futile creek whose bottom was moist sixty days out of every three hundred and sixty-five. Yet Dryfooting could point with pride to a railroad spur that connected it with the outside world, a ponderous edifice known as the Grand Opera House, and the only hotel in that part of Montana called the Seraglio.

Said Bert Beecham, its rotund and heavy-thighed proprietor, who'd gotten the name from a book: "I don't rightly know what the word means, but it shore is purty."

To Dryfooting came Rowdy Dow and Stumpy Grampis in the late afternoon, having followed a circuitous trail from the rimrock many miles to the north. They had ridden warily, ever mindful that behind them was a girl with an uncanny knack for placing a rifle shot in the right or wrong place—depending upon the viewpoint—and also that ahead of them was a man with a broken spur and a flour sack hood who had every reason to ambush them if circumstances permitted. Also, they had remembered that the gentleman had friends. His associates had been heading north when last sighted, but perhaps they'd circled to join the one who'd stolen the saddle. Rowdy had his private opinion of full-grown men who ran around with flour sacks pulled over their heads, but all the signs said that that crew played for keeps.

Thus Rowdy had ridden with his hand close to his holster, and Stumpy had been equally alert, but they'd sighted no one in that jumbled country. Within an hour Rowdy might have believed that the whole episode of the rimrock had been a bad dream, except that the burlap-wrapped saddle offered ever-present proof of the reality of the adventure. Rowdy pined mightily to have a look at that saddle. He'd hoped to ask the sharp-shooting young lady just what made the kak so valuable, but the girl had seemed to speak only one kind of language, and Rowdy knew better than to palaver with a Winchester. Now there was nothing to do but tote the saddle to Dryfooting and turn it over to the law.

But even that feat proved to be beset by difficulties. In the town and with their horses stabled at the livery, the two clanked their spurs into the lobby of the Seraglio, Rowdy still toting the saddle. Here they signed the register with bold flourishes lest Caleb Hackett be the kind who couldn't see well without his glasses. To Bert Beecham, who presided behind the desk, Rowdy said, "And where will we find the sheriff, my fat friend?"

"Sheriff rode out into the badlands this morning," Beecham replied. "The Winged-H reported some rustling again. Reckon this town will be doing without law today."

Rowdy sighed. "Show us our room."

A creaking, carpeted stairway led upward to the room, one of many that flanked a dim and musty hallway, and the room itself was not the kind to remind a man that the dictionary's definition of a seraglio was "any resort of debauchery; a place of licentious pleasure." This room, instead, was so plainly furnished that it would have gladdened the eye of the most zealous missionary; obviously one night in its chipped bed would make a martyr out of the occupant, and the chair looked like an instrument of the Inquisition. But the cracked pitcher and bowl were serviceable, and Rowdy sloshed water from the one to the other, delved into the warsack which Stumpy had hauled along, and proceeded to shave himself. This done, Rowdy said, "Let's eat."

They locked the door behind them, and Rowdy pocketed the key, but before they found a restaurant to their liking, they came abreast of the Grand Opera House and before this ancient fire-trap, Rowdy paused, tugging at Stumpy's elbow. Huge posters fronted the place, and Rowdy indicated one with a jab of his thumb. "Take a look," he urged. "Does this tell you anything?"

The poster read:

NATHANIEL FAUST PRESENTS
An Outstanding Programme of Entertainment
For Young & Old

The Evening's Entertainment Will Commence
With the Laughable Farce
THE MAID'S NIGHT OFF
Barnaby Squires . . . . Nathaniel Faust
Chloe, a colored maid . . . . Nan Bolton

OVERTURE . . . . Banjo Selections
MISS NAN BOLTON
Pronounced by the Press and Public to Be
THE GREATEST SHARPSHOOTER OF ALL TIME!

The World Renowned PROFESSOR MARVELO
In Feats of Magic and Legerdemain
I*N*C*L*U*D*I*N*G
THE DEVIL'S SADDLE!
See It Disappear Before Your Very Eyes!

CORONET SOLO .... NATHANIEL FAUST

The Whole to Conclude With a Laughable Sketch
Entitled:
DOES YOUR MOTHER KNOW YOU'RE OUT?
Mr. Digby .... Nathaniel Faust
Susie Prescott .... Nan Bolton
Other Characters by the Company

"The Company," Rowdy decided, "must be the six
horses that were hauling that fancy-painted stagecoach.
So they're show people. No wonder that gal could make a
rifle talk. 'The greatest sharpshooter of all time!' You've
got to admit that that takes in territory, Stumpy."

"Nathaniel Faust and Professor Marvelo must be the
same gent," Stumpy decided. "The feller with the white
whiskers. Rowdy, you reckon we'll get a couple of free
passes to the show when we return that saddle?"

"More likely we'll get our pants dusted by the world's
greatest sharpshooter," Rowdy opined. "So they use the
saddle in a magic act. Well, I can believe that part of the
bill. Already the saddle's disappeared before Professor
Marvelo's very eyes. But I still don't savvy why the kak
was stolen."

"Let's eat," Stumpy growled. "My stomach feels like
my mouth has taken a pasear to Texas and left it behind."

They shouldered into a restaurant and lingered over
steak and fried spuds and apple pie and coffee, and all the
while Rowdy was studying Dryfooting and its populace. If
Caleb Hackett's mysterious proposition kept him sojourn-
ing here, he might need to know this town. Dryfooting
seemed gripped in a lasting somnolence, and such of its
citizens as were in the restaurant were a dispirited lot.
But Rowdy knew these cowtowns. They came to life when

the sun went down; and Dryfooting, he'd observed, had its full share of saloons. And when the two came again to the boardwalk before the restaurant, they found a flurry of excitement.

Dust boiled as a half-dozen horses came down the street, and, the band swirling by, Rowdy saw that they were wild cayuses with only the first roughness worn off them in some remote badlands breaking corral. But it was the man who hazed them along who held Rowdy's eye.

"Checkered Shirt," Stumpy breathed, thereby revealing that he was equally alert. "Rowdy, it looks like if you wait long enough, sooner or later everybody in the world comes to Dryfooting."

"Who's the wrangler?" Rowdy asked of a boardwalk loiterer.

"Calls hisself the Rimrock Kid," he was told. "Traps those broomtails in the badlands, takes the kinks out of 'em, and hazes 'em here to the loading pens."

The Rimrock Kid had gone flashing by, but Rowdy had gotten a better glimpse of him than he'd had when he'd watched this same Kid come to the rescue of Nan Bolton and Nathaniel Faust, out in the badlands. The Kid was young, no more than twenty-one or -two, and saddlewhacking had thinned him to a wiry hardness, and badlands suns had given him the hue of old leather. There was a certain devil-may-care recklessness in him, manifested by a ready grin that showed startlingly white teeth. But that grin had been impersonal; the Kid's dark eye had shown no sign of recognition as he'd passed Rowdy and Stumpy.

"I'd like a word with him," Rowdy murmured. "Hosses used to be my line."

"He'll haze those broomtails to the tracks," the loiterer said. "Then he'll likely have a drink at the Tarantula to celebrate a day's work done. You'll find him there."

"Come along, Stumpy," Rowdy said, for he'd already marked the shingle of the Tarantula Saloon.

Crossing the street which was still astir with the passage of those many unshod hoofs, Rowdy wondered exactly what he did mean to say to the Rimrock Kid. This whole affair was none of his; he'd come here on a matter involving a certain Caleb Hackett, and what had happened in the badlands was presumably finished business as far as he, Rowdy, was concerned. Yet he wanted to know how the girl and her aged companion had fared with their broken stagecoach, and, if the Rimrock Kid was a friend of Nan Bolton's, as seemed to be the case, Rowdy wanted to leave word as to where she'd find her vanished saddle. This much Rowdy admitted to himself. The truth was that a consuming curiosity was egging him on.

The Tarantula was apparently Dryfooting's largest saloon. Even at this early hour its hitchrail was crowded with cayuses, and among them Rowdy noticed some that bore the Winged-H brand. He wondered where he'd heard of that spread until he remembered that the hotel man had mentioned it earlier today. Shouldering through the batwings, Rowdy saw a long bar, an expanse of sawdust-sprinkled floor, a scattering of tables and chairs. Bellied up to the bar were six men, elbow to elbow, and these paid scant heed to the partners' entrance. Or so Rowdy thought until he realized that he and Stumpy had been observed in the bar mirror and that, with the looking-glass before them, the men at the bar could watch the batwings surreptitiously. Rowdy seated himself at a table near the rear of the room, picked a chair that put his back to the wall and signaled Stumpy to be seated.

Stumpy obeyed with alacrity, his leathery face showing the first enthusiasm he'd displayed since leaving the Little Belts. But this elation vanished when the aproned bartender came around to take their order. Stumpy had his mouth all puckered to say, "Whiskey," but Rowdy was quicker of tongue. "Beer," Rowdy said firmly. "A couple of bottles of beer."

"I been recollectin'," Stumpy said plaintively. "This must just about be my birthday, the way I calculate it. Now, considering the occasion, a little festivity wouldn't be unseemly, now would it? I was thinkin'—"

"You had a birthday," Rowdy reminded him, "just a month ago. The day we left the cabin to get supplies, remember. And you had another birthday just before we holed-up last fall. Which means that you're not going to have another birthday for at least a month."

The beer placed before them, Stumpy solaced himself with the amber fluid, but Rowdy, sipping his slowly, took to studying the group at the bar. A hardcase lot, he decided, but one, near the center of the sextet, was the most sinister, a big-boned, heavily muscled man whose dark and swarthy face Rowdy could glimpse in the bar mirror. The fellow affected a ragged mustache, and there was a tiny scar on his left cheekbone. This man had been watching Rowdy in the mirror, but, aware now of Rowdy's attention, the fellow dropped his eyes to the whiskey glass he held between blunt finger and thumb. It made Rowdy uncomfortable, this scrutiny he'd been receiving, but he shrugged the feeling aside. Strangers in a strange town were apt to be inspected upon arrival.

"Here's your man," Stumpy suddenly announced. "Just come in."

The batwings had parted to the shoulders of the Rimrock Kid, and the Kid was striding into the saloon, beating the dust from his chaps with his sombrero. It was Rowdy's thought to hail him to his table and offer him a drink as a means of introduction, but he never got to make the gesture. The six at the bar had noticed the Kid's entry, too; the big man with the ragged mustache had nudged his closest companion, and now, without a word, the two at either end of the group faded away from the bar, cutting across Rimrock's path of travel and taking one of the tables not far from Rowdy and Stumpy.

Whereupon the big man who was left at the bar with three companions turned now, putting his back to the mirror and propping his elbows on the edge of the mahogany. With studied insolence he said, "Howdy, Kid. Brought some more broomtails into town, they tell me. I heard you were quitting hosses because you'd got mighty interested in cattle. Winged-H cattle."

The Kid stopped dead in his tracks, a quick flush of red mantling his face and a ready anger leaping into his eyes. "Kelhorn," he said, "this ain't the first time you've accused me of rustling Winged-H beef. But it's the first time you've said it to my face. And it will be the last!"

The challenge was there, plain for any man to hear; and Kelhorn's three companions took quick sideways steps away from the big man until the four were neatly spaced out along the bar. But it was the two who'd meandered to a far table that Rowdy was watching. Those two had seated themselves, but they'd moved their chairs back from the table, and their feet were drawn up under them so that only their boot toes touched the floor. They were ready and waiting, taut as coiled springs. Thus the trap had been rigged; the Rimrock Kid had Winged-H men on either side of him; they pocketed their prey so that the Kid would be caught in a crossfire when the guns began blasting. But the Kid was too blind with anger to see this.

Not so Rowdy Dow. Nor Stumpy either. Stumpy was quietly easing his chair around so that he could come to a stand quickly, and, though no word passed between the partners, each understood that they were taking a hand in this. What happened to the impetuous Rimrock Kid was no skin off their noses, but the smell of a gun-trap could be sickening, and both Rowdy and Stumpy had gotten more than a good whiff. But still the impetus to action had to come from the Kid—that would be essential when Dryfooting's law later demanded an accounting—and Kelhorn used words now as a man might use a lash.

"I say you're a sneaking dark-o'-the-moon cow thief, Kid," Kelhorn snapped. "I say that you could tell where every cow that's been missing from the Winged-H these last few weeks has gone to. I say it to your face, and I'm asking what you're going to do about it!"

"*This!*" the Kid shouted, and his hand fell toward his holster.

That was when Rowdy jumped. Not toward the Kid, nor toward Kelhorn and the others at the bar, but toward the table where two more Winged-H hands were already reaching for guns. Rowdy made it to that table in a bound, grasping its rounded edge and heaving upward and sideward. The two behind the table had not quite gotten to their feet. Their guns were half out of holsters when the edge of the table caught them across their chests and sent them bowling over backward, their chairs splintering beneath them. But with these two rendered *hors de combat* for the moment, the saloon had become a thundering inferno of roaring guns.

Six men were firing; the four at the bar, the Rimrock Kid, and Stumpy Grampis. Stumpy, seeing Rowdy's move which had temporarily taken care of the two at the table, had unlimbered his gun, and Stumpy's lead, splintering the top of the bar, had given the Winged-H quartet a sudden awareness that outside help had bought in on the side of the Rimrock Kid. And that was the Kid's saving. The four had fanned wider apart as Stumpy's gun barked; two of them hastily heaved themselves onto the bar and went sliding across it, bobbing out of sight behind the mahogany where the bartender had already disappeared.

And the Kid was a weaving, dodging shadow of a man, dancing backward toward the batwings.

"*Get out of here, Kid!*" Rowdy shouted. "*They've stacked the odds!*"

The Kid shot one hasty glance toward Rowdy, another toward the two Winged-H men who were clambering to their feet from beneath the overturned table. His first true realization of the situation seemed to penetrate his consciousness, and he flashed a look at Rowdy that was pure gratefulness and was gone through the batwings. The bartender heaved into view; in his pudgy fists was a sawed-off shotgun which he swung in a wide arc, bellowing the while: "Stand your hands, all of you! You're not wrecking *my* place tonight!"

That menacing shotgun froze everyone momentarily. But Rowdy had spied a rear doorway, and he got Stumpy by the elbow and shoved him toward it. The bartender was content to let them go, but Winged-H lead bid them an angry adieu, driving splinters from the door jamb as the partners went through the opening. They stumbled across a room littered with cased whiskey and beer barrels, found another door and clawed it open, then dodged along a dusk-dimmed alley.

"Half a dozen guns barking and no blood spilled," Rowdy panted as they finally came to a stop. "The West is turning tame, old hoss."

But a towering rage had laid hold of Stumpy Grampis. "My beer," he moaned. "It weren't even half drunk. And one of them Winged-H galoots busted the bottle with the first shot he sent at me. Dang the murderin' sons! Dang their blasted hides!"

"We'd better get back to the hotel and go to bed," Rowdy suggested. "We've had a mighty busy day."

3

THE SNAKE BRAND

Over on the street hoofs sired a wild flurry of sound, and that, Rowdy judged, was the Rimrock Kid making discretion the better part of valor. A rash impetuousness had brought the wild horse hunter to the brink of Boothill, but the Kid was now shaking the dust of Dryfooting, which meant that the questions Rowdy had intended to ask would go unanswered tonight. Or so Rowdy thought. Then the Kid, a fine figure in a saddle, was cutting between two buildings and finding his way into the alley, his eyes questing avidly. Sighting the partners, he hauled to a stop.

"*Gracias, amigos,*" he said softly. "I waited beyond the batwings long enough to make sure that you two had skinned out of that snakes' nest. Seems I owe you my hide."

"They had you stacked," Rowdy conceded. "What was behind the ruckus?"

"You're strangers," the Kid instantly decided. He cast a long look down the alley toward the rear door of the Tarantula, and there was nobody to be seen. He cocked an ear toward the main street; it was silent save for the normal sounds of the evening. "The Winged-H is the biggest ranch hereabouts," he said. "Somebody's been cutting out cattle of nights and hazing them deeper into the badlands. Me, I pick up a dollar or two trapping wild horses, working the rough off 'em, and selling the broomtails. Jake Kelhorn, Winged-H's segundo, has got it in his head that I might be the gent who's walking off with those cows."

Rowdy grinned. "And there wouldn't be a lick of truth to that?"

The same heady anger the Kid had displayed in the

Tarantula darkened his face again. This Kid was pepper-skinned and hair-triggered, Rowdy decided, but the youngster's moods were transitory, for his anger was only fleeting. He matched Rowdy's grin. "I'll take that," the Kid said. "From you. No, I'm no rustler, mister. And I'm beholden to you. What do you call yourself?"

"Rowdy Dow. And this stove-up example of what comes of a wasted youth is Stumpy Grampis."

The Kid's dark eyes flashed. "I've heard of the pair of you. The papers had something to say of a job of work you did in Latigo Basin last fall. Riding through?"

Rowdy ignored the question. "We've met you before, sort of," he said. "We were up on the rimrock when you were helping a girl and an old man in a fancy stagecoach stand off a bunch of hooded galoots. We couldn't find a trail and get down to take cards. The girl and the old man friends of yours?"

"Never saw 'em before today," the Kid said. "I was up on the far slope when I found myself with a grandstand seat to the big race. When the coach busted a wheel, I saw that the two of 'em were in the middle of a hornets' nest. So I bought in. They're show people, and they're playing Dryfooting as soon as they can get here. I sent the blacksmith out tonight with a spare wheel for 'em. It was the best I could do."

"You don't figger those masked gents are likely to come back at them while the two are sitting out in the badlands waiting for a replacement wheel?"

The Kid shook his head. "The girl didn't think so. I offered to bring her in aboard my horse, but she wanted to stick with the old fellow. He's her granddad. Those raiders got what they were after—a saddle the old man uses in a magic act."

"The saddle is up in our hotel room," Rowdy said. "When that one jasper made off with it, he climbed right up to us. We tangled our twine at trying to bag him, but we did get the saddle. I figured on giving it back to the girl then, but she was seeing enemies everywhere. I wasn't arguing with her Winchester."

The Kid gave Rowdy a long appraisal. "You're the gent all right," he conceded. "I didn't get much of a look at you when you showed on the rim with the saddle in your arms, but I did see that you weren't wearing a hood. I tried to tell the girl that you weren't the galoot who'd took off with the saddle, but she was mad plumb through, and she wouldn't listen. Fact is, I had a hard time talking her out of climbing the slope on foot. She's mighty pretty, that girl is, but she's got a temper. Gawd pity the galoot who marries her!"

"Anyway, she gets her saddle back when she gets to town," Rowdy said. "Any idea who those masked jiggers were?"

"They were riding unbranded horses—which might mean everything or nothing," the Kid said. "They could have had other horses stashed out in a badlands corral and changed mounts before and after the ruckus. No, I can't put the Injun sign on 'em."

Again he glanced up the alley and cocked an ear toward the street. "I'll be moseying along now," he said. "Jake Kelhorn is a man who hates hard. I'm sorry that he'll be hating you two from here on out on my account."

"We'll bear up under it," Rowdy said. "Good luck, Kid."

"*Gracias, amigos,*" the Kid said again, and, wheeling his horse up the alley, he was gone. Rowdy looked after him for a long moment, and then said, "Come on, Stumpy. Time a feller of your tender years was in bed."

Whereupon the two cut between the buildings and came again to the boardwalk, sending a swift, backward glance toward the Tarantula and seeing nothing to concern them. The Winged-H saddlers were still before the saloon, Rowdy judged, which indicated that Jake Kelhorn and his hardcase crew had decided against pursuit of either the Rimrock Kid or the two who'd sided the wild horse hunter. A few minutes later the partners were climbing the carpeted stairway of the Seraglio, and Stumpy, breaking a long silence, said, "We're improving, Rowdy. That Rimrock Kid will side us from hell to breakfast now, which same means that we've made one friend in this country—and only about two dozen enemies. I hope I don't never meet that Jake Kelhorn in the dark. He's plumb poison!"

"See what you get for talking about the devil," Rowdy said and made a gesture with his thumb.

They'd reached the head of the stairs now, and they could see the long hallway, dimly lighted by overhanging coal-oil lamps, and there, ahead of them, leaning against their locked door was the big-boned figure of Jake Kelhorn, arms folded. Stumpy Grampis took one look, made a quick, sideward step, and dropped his hand toward his gun. But Kelhorn only smiled, a peeling back of lips from teeth. "Nothing to get excited about, gents," he said. "I'm here on business."

"Monkey business!" Stumpy muttered.

"Let's go inside," Kelhorn said. "If you're worried, you can lift my gun out of leather."

Rowdy spoke from the corner of his mouth as they advanced down the hall. "You said it was your birthday, Stumpy. How do you like this? A surprise party."

But at the same time he was fishing his key from his pocket, and, as Kelhorn stepped aside, Rowdy fitted the key into the door and swung the portal inward, beckoning to Kelhorn to enter. Kelhorn's presence here made no more sense than a Chinese laundry ticket, but, as long as Winged-H's segundo was sprouting olive branches, there was nothing to be gained by belligerency. Into the room, Rowdy lighted the lamp on the bureau, turning his back on Kelhorn as he performed the operation, but knowing that Stumpy was meanwhile keeping a wary eye on the man. The lamp burning, Rowdy indicated the chair. "Sit down," he said.

Kelhorn obeyed, hoisting his legs to the bedstead and crossing them there. "You're Rowdy Dow and Stumpy Grampis," he said. "I found your names on the register not more than five minutes ago. Naturally, I didn't know you down at the Tarantula, and you didn't know me. I ain't holding it against you for buying in on the Kid's side. You're strangers here, and you don't savvy that we treat rustlers like any other kind of snake. The Kid's slippery. We didn't dare take chances."

Stumpy had gingerly seated himself upon the edge of the bed; Rowdy squatted on his heels near the burlap-wrapped saddle. Spreading his hands in a gesture that dismissed the past, Rowdy said, "All right, Kelhorn. You're willing to let bygones be bygones, and we've got no grudge. But that doesn't explain why you're here. Get it out of you, mister."

"I'm representing my boss, Caleb Hackett, the owner of the Winged-H," Kelhorn said. "You got his letter, I reckon. Every time I've ridden to town, I've had a look at the Seraglio's register, hoping to find you here."

Rowdy tried not to show his surprise. "So you're Hackett's foreman," he said. "Seems to be a mighty small world."

"Gettin' stuffy, if you ask me," Stumpy said sourly.

"I'm Hackett's foreman," Kelhorn said. "And I handle most of his business for him. Hackett's an old man, and he doesn't sit a saddle as well as he used to. Likewise, he has an old man's whims, and he can change his mind mighty quick. I'm sorry to say that you've had a long ride for nothing. The boss isn't going to need your services. He asked me to find out if a hundred dollars would square it for the trouble he's put you to."

Rowdy leaned forward. "You mean we're to take a hundred dollars and forget the whole business? The deal's off?"

Kelhorn thrust a hand into a pocket, produced a roll of currency, and peeled off a hundred dollar bill. "That's the idea," he said. "You willing to accept?"

"Hackett's letter spoke of cutting us in on a share of some lost gold," Rowdy said. "A hundred dollars is fair enough for all we've done so far, but it isn't what we were expecting. It's mighty disappointing to have things turn out this way."

Kelhorn smiled again, the whiteness of his teeth showing fleetingly in his swarthy face. "Griffen's Gold has been hunted by many men, Dow. A feller of your experience knows how those hidden treasure stories go. I ain't saying nothing against Caleb Hackett, seeing as I'm drawing his pay. But I've told you that he's an old man. Let's say that once in a while he gets a delusion."

"Just like that uncle o' mine!" Stumpy interjected. "Took to climbing up on the highest ridgepoles and braying like a doggone jackass. Claimed it was the mating season for mountain canaries and nobody could budge him out of the notion."

Rowdy shrugged, his eyes on Kelhorn. "Hackett hired us, so I guess it's his right to fire us." Coming to a stand, he reached for the bill which Kelhorn extended. "Tell your boss there's no hard feelings," Rowdy added.

Kelhorn lowered his spurs to the floor and likewise got to his feet. "No hard feelings here, either," he said. "In fact, if you'll come back to the Tarantula, I'll buy the drinks."

Stumpy instantly displayed a great eagerness, but it was

Rowdy's thought that affability did not set well on the broad shoulders of Jake Kelhorn. In the Tarantula, rigging a gun-trap to bag the Rimrock Kid, Winged-H's foreman had been much more in his element than in this room where he'd played the diplomat for his absent boss. Rowdy said, "Thanks, just the same. It's a long way back to the Little Belts and we'll be riding out early. Which means we'll be hitting the hay pronto."

Kelhorn stepped toward the door, paused, and let his eyes drop to the burlap-wrapped saddle. "Looks like you gents are toting an extra hull," he said. "Care to sell it? Mine's got to the point where haywire won't hold it together."

"The saddle," Rowdy said, "isn't ours. We'll be leaving it at the sheriff's office before we ride out, and its rightful owner can claim it there. How we come by it is a long story, and likely you'd find it a dull one, Kelhorn. No sale."

Kelhorn put his hand to the doorknob. "No harm in asking. I'll be getting along. It's been mighty nice meeting gents of your rep. We've heard of you, Dow, even back here in the badlands. So long."

He eased out into the hallway, his boots beat along the carpet to the stairs; and Stumpy spread-eagled himself across the bed then, his leathery face jubilant. "So you had to come ridin' half-way across Montana on account of that ding-busted letter!" he said. "I told you, remember, that Hackett would likely turn out to be loonier than a hooty owl. Let's get to bed, Rowdy. Me, I'm pining to look through my cayuse's ears in the direction of the Little Belts."

Rowdy was picking up the chair and propping it firmly under the doorknob, and he said, "You won't be doing much snoozing tonight, old hoss. You and me are taking turns sitting up with yonder saddle. Before this night's over, somebody is going to make a play at taking it away from us."

"Kelhorn?" Stumpy snorted loudly. "Just because he wanted to buy it, do you think he'll come back and steal it? He doesn't have to steal anything. You see that roll of *dinero* he was packing? An ox couldn't wash it down with a barrel o' water!"

"Mr. Kelhorn," Rowdy said patiently, "recognized us when we came into the Tarantula this evening, and that's why he kept watching us in the bar mirror. No, he didn't recognize us as Rowdy Dow and Stumpy Grampis, those famous jackasses who were coming in answer to Caleb Hackett's letter. He was probably plumb surprised when he found our names on the hotel register tonight and then realized that we were the pair he'd just been trying to smoke down. But, in the saloon, he did recognize us as the two gents who'd been on the rimrock and had gotten The Devil's Saddle away from him. Naturally, he couldn't let on that he'd recognized us. That would have put him in a mighty awkward spot. But recognize us he did."

"Meaning—?" Stumpy demanded.

"Meaning that we'll be riding out of here tomorrow morning, just like I told him. But we won't be heading for the Little Belts. We'll be having a look-see at the Winged-H, and a palaver with Caleb Hackett. Me, I don't think Mr. Hackett changed his mind about wanting our services. That was Jake Kelhorn's way of getting rid of us."

Stumpy sat bolt upright. "But why should Kelhorn be passing out money in his boss' name just to head us out of here?"

"I don't know," Rowdy admitted. "But I do know that Kelhorn's got the snake brand stamped all over him. Did you notice his boots when he hoisted them to the top of the bed while he was sitting here? One of his spurs was

broken. I saw that same spur earlier today. Out in the
badlands when we tried to trip up Jake Kelhorn after he'd
stolen a saddle from those show people. You were right,
Stumpy, when you said that if you waited long enough,
sooner or later everybody in the world would come to
Dryfooting. We've had a busy day, but likely we'll have a
busier night. Kelhorn wants that saddle. And, if I'm any
judge, Kelhorn will come after it."

RAIDERS NOCTURNAL

Night came discordantly to Dryfooting. There was no po-
etic falling of the shades in muted, murmuring silence, no
soothing departure of the cares that infest the day. Quite
the contrary. Dryfooting, like some gaunt, gray tomcat
that had slept through the sunlight, was now stretching
itself, flexing its claws, and getting ready to make moon-
music. The rutted street, so dispirited in the daytime, echoed a constant thunder of hoofs as riders larruped in from
outlying badlands ranches, the horse and rope men sali-
vating the sky with raucous six-shooters and announcing
to all and sundry that they were curly wolves whose time
had come to howl. Saloons that had been listless came to
strident life. Tinny pianos merged a tuneless medley;
boardwalks knew the beat of many boots; hitchrails were
crowded to capacity. The lid was off.

With this symphony of unlovely sound percolating
through the thin planking of the Seraglio, Rowdy and
Stumpy prepared for their night-long vigil. Rowdy had a
look from the one window of the room, a window facing
on the side of the building, and discovered that it gave
him an oblique glimpse of the street. Directly below was

an open space between this building and the next, a narrow slot littered with debris. From the window to the ground was a straight drop, and this Rowdy noted with satisfaction. An intruder would need wings to gain the room by way of the window.

That meant that the door would likely suffer any assault that was made, and, with the door locked and the chair propped under its knob, an intruder would certainly announce himself if he tried entering by force. Rowdy sighed, realizing that he'd let his nerves get keyed up to a pitch of anticipation. Whatever was going to happen would probably not happen until hours later. Raiders would wait until the town had quieted and it might safely be presumed that the occupants of the Seraglio were asleep.

Turning to the burlap-wrapped saddle that was keeping him awake, Rowdy fell to examining the object. The burlap, he'd already noted, was laced shut by twine; now he discovered that it would be a simple matter to remove the saddle from its wrapping and restore it afterward. But this was to be expected. Nathaniel Faust used the hull in his act, which meant that the saddle was unpacked and packed from town to town. His curiosity consuming him, Rowdy fumbled at the twine and soon had the burlap removed.

"Just a plain ole kak," Stumpy said in great disappointment, peering over Rowdy's shoulder.

And so it was. A stock saddle, heavy, broad, and double-cinched, it was worn with use. Its stirrups had ponderous tapaderos, designed to keep a rider from pushing his feet through and snagging them in brush; its horn was built for tying rather than dallying. A rimfire Texican saddle. There was no fancy inlaid work of gold or silver or ivory: nothing to give this saddle a value over and above a thousand other hulls of like construction and vintage. Yet men had put forth savage effort today to lay their hands upon it, and Rowdy, frowning at this object of leather and wood, wished it could talk.

"Whatever makes it valuable isn't showing on the outside," he remarked.

"Let's tear it apart," Stumpy said quickly.

Rowdy pulled the burlap covering back over the kak and began lacing it shut. "And get ourselves up to our ears in trouble when those show people reach town? Remember, Stumpy, we told the Rimrock Kid that we got this kak, and we likewise told him that we were returning it. I reckon it better go back in the same shape we got it."

Stumpy, plainly disappointed, spread-eagled himself upon the bed again, and Rowdy added: "You might as well grab some sleep. I'll wake you later and let you have a turn at keeping watch."

"Ain't gonna sleep a wink," Stumpy announced. "If there's any excitement, I aim to be in on it."

Ten minutes later he was snoring lustily. Rowdy tiptoed to the lamp, blew out the flame, then seated himself upon the floor in a corner and began his vigil. He built many cigarettes and smoked them; he listened to the raucous night life of Dryfooting, marking its rise to its greatest pitch before it began to dwindle as some cowboys, patently aware that morning came early, began riding out of town. The hotel had quieted down; in the next room a late-comer prepared for sleep, and Rowdy plainly heard the creak of springs as the fellow seated himself on the edge of his bed. A boot thudded to the floor as the man dropped it; Rowdy waited in tense eagerness for the fall of the second boot and was about convinced that their neighbor was a one-legged man when he was rewarded by the thud of the other boot. Shortly the bed springs creaked again as the fellow settled himself for the night.

An hour had gone by, and another and another. Now it

was past midnight and the street was growing comparatively quiet. Two drunks went lurching up the boardwalk, supporting each other and attempting harmony on a song having to do with a miner, forty-niner, and his daughter, Clem-en-t-i-i-ne. A horse plodded quietly, making soft noises in the dust. A lone piano tinkled discordantly, the sound remote and sometimes lost. Rowdy spun another cigarette, smoked it until his fingers were scorched, and stubbed it out upon the floor.

After that, he slept. He had no remembrance of dozing; he found his chin upon his chest much later, and awoke with a start. The moon was aloft and high enough so that some of its light seeped in through the window, laying the rectangular pattern of the sash upon the faded carpet. Rowdy could make out the bed, the bureau with its cracked bowl and pitcher, the chair tilted beneath the doorknob. His partner was still snoring, but not so lustily; the sound a soft, wheezy effort that began as a whistle and ended as a sob. A mouse ventured forth from a dark corner, surveyed Rowdy in beady-eyed fascination, and went scurrying under the bureau. The town was silent.

Yet some sound had awakened Rowdy. This he knew with an instinct developed in days when his picture had adorned reward dodgers and certain sheriffs had made a career of trying to corner him. He searched for that sound, expecting that it would be in the hallway beyond the door, and then he heard a faint scraping. It came to him with a start that the sound was being made at the window sill. The sash had been raised a few inches. Rowdy tried hard to remember whether it had been this way all the time and decided that it had. Stumpy had wanted ventilation.

Rowdy began moving, his actions studiously slow, his intent being to get to his feet. Muscles cramped by his hours of vigil protested, and, when he stood erect, needles shuttled in one of his feet which had gone asleep. He inched toward the window, his eyes and ears sharpened to the needs of the moment, and, keeping to one side of the frame, he got a look outside without showing himself. Below lay a muddy darkness; the moon was not yet high enough to cast its light into the void between the two buildings, yet Rowdy was certain that he made out movement, dim and furtive, down there. And instantly he realized the meaning of that movement. The scraping sound was repeated, and he saw that a ladder was being carefully raised to the window.

This was the unexpected—the attack coming by the one way that had seemed unassailable. Very carefully Rowdy drew his gun and stood waiting. The top of the ladder seemed to search, tentatively, for the window sill, and, finding it, settled there. Down below, voices murmured softly; the ladder creaked as a man put his weight to it. Still Rowdy did nothing, merely standing, merely waiting. It took forever for that man to mount the ladder; Rowdy would have sworn that at least ten minutes went by before he glimpsed the intruder. Then he made out the head and shoulders of a man and saw the high, pointed outline of the hood masking the fellow.

The man was leaning his body against the ladder and putting his hands to hoisting the sash. He did this slowly, inch by inch, pausing after each protesting sound and apparently listening intently. He was many minutes at this task, and it was an interminable time before he had the sash high enough to admit the passage of his body into the room. He stepped up to the next rung then, thrust his head and shoulders through the opening—and Rowdy elected to move.

One step brought him from where he'd flattened against the wall to a stand before the window. And as he stepped, he was swinging his gun. The long barrel lifted and descended, smashing down against the point of the raider's hood and crumpling it, and the man sagged, stunned but not quite unconscious. The fellow must have fallen the length of his body before some wavering instinct sent his hands in search of a staying hold. Rowdy risked leaning from the window; he saw the fellow clutching dazedly at the ladder, saw the man slide again, clutch again, and then go tumbling on down toward the ground. The darkness swallowed the man, but Rowdy heard the thud as the fellow lighted below. Muted curses drifted upward as those who'd helped hoist the ladder clustered around the fallen one.

Rowdy hastily withdrew into the room, mindful that with the moonlight touching him he'd made a fine target. He supposed they'd be trying the ladder again, coming up in a swarm and prepared to overwhelm him in one ruthless rush. But suddenly the top of the ladder was no longer visible; it scraped against the side of the building, and there was a flurry of movement down in the darkness, and then silence clamped upon the shadowed areaway.

They had gone, taking their ladder with them. They had tried and failed and were trying no more—at least not by the means they'd just employed. The episode was over, and all of it had happened in such silence that it was like a dream vaguely remembered. The fall of the intruder from the ladder had aroused no one; Stumpy still snored softly, and so did the man in the next room. Pouching the gun he'd wielded so effectively, Rowdy crossed over to his partner and shook him gently. Stumpy came awake with a start, sitting upright, and Rowdy made a gesture beseeching silence.

"We've had company," Rowdy whispered. "The flour sack boys were here."

"Where are they?" Stumpy demanded wildly and began probing the floor beside the bed for the gun-belt he'd discarded prior to stretching out. "Let me at the misguided sons!"

"They're gone," Rowdy explained and told all that had transpired. Stumpy heard him out in sullen silence. "You could 'a' woke me when you fust heard 'em," Stumpy complained. "You didn't need to go hoggin' all the fun."

"And had you hop out of bed like the hotel was on fire? It was too risky. But I don't reckon the deal's over. They'll make another try. They gave up too easy to suit me."

Stumpy swung his legs to the floor. "I ain't missin' out the next time," he announced. "You can help yourself to some shut-eye, if you like. Me, I'm keeping guard."

But Rowdy elected to stay awake. The two hunkered in separate corners, saying nothing and sometimes fashioning cigarettes whose red eyes winked in the darkness. The moonlight faded, and the mouse, emboldened by the silence, ventured across the room and went rustling under the bed. An hour went by, a long, endless hour, and Rowdy said, "Must be near morning. Maybe they *did* get a bellyful."

Shortly after that he dozed again. And, as on the earlier occasion, he was aroused by some sound percolating into that part of his consciousness which remained forever on guard. He came awake to find Stumpy standing rigid in the middle of the room. Stumpy heard the slight movement of Rowdy's awakening and turned his leathery old face in the younger man's direction, one finger raised to his straggly mustache. In Stumpy's right hand was his gun. Stumpy gestured with a nod of his head toward the door, and Rowdy, peering hard, saw that the handle was slowly and silently turning.

Here was the expected. The attempt to enter by way of the window had failed, therefore it followed that any second attempt would be made at the door. A sufficient amount of time had been allowed to elapse to put the partners off their guard, and now the intruders were try-ing again. Or so Rowdy saw it. But Stumpy—bless his wary old soul—had not been caught napping. Stumpy had heard movement out in the hallway, and Stumpy was pre-pared.

More so than Rowdy suspected. Whoever had put their hand to the doorknob had discovered that the door was locked, and now the intruder was probing at the keyhole. These hotel doors were usually locked by a skeleton key, and many a man—Rowdy included—carried one. The chair was still propped under the knob, but a concerted rush of men would sweep that flimsy barrier away. And doubtless that was the strategy of the hooded men. They intended to pile pell-mell into the room, snatch the saddle and be gone while the partners were pawing the sleep from their eyes.

But if that were the case, they had not reckoned with the wariness of Stumpy Grampis. Nor with his belligerent nature.

Rowdy's strategy would have been to wait, to have given them their chance at rushing the door and then to have prepared a hot welcome. Not so Stumpy. He had missed out on the first attempt at invasion, and he was not going to have his fun spoiled a second time. The key rattling in the door, Stumpy hoisted his gun. And before Rowdy could make a move, Stumpy's gun blared, the roar of it thunderous in the confines of the room, the lead drilling a hole through the doorway at approximately the height of a tall man's head.

"Take that!" Stumpy bellowed. "Take that and let it be a lesson! It's just the start of what you're gonna get!"

The hotel came alive. Bed springs creaked in the rooms on either side of this one; sleepy voices raised in startled ejaculation; but above all the bedlam of a building aroused, the two heard the rattle of the doorknob. "Open up!" a voice demanded—a hoarse voice that might best be described as a whiskey baritone. "Open up, I say! I'll teach you two saddle-stealing sons a thing or two! Shoot a hole through my hat, will you!"

Rowdy was on his feet. "Who's there?" he demanded.

"McCandless," the hoarse voice retorted. "Who do you think it is? The Queen of Sheba? Open up, damn it. I'm dragging the pair of you down to jail. I'll teach you to go shooting at the sheriff of this county. Open up!"

Rowdy looked dismally at his partner who was staring at the gun in his hand as though it had suddenly sprouted scales and a forked tongue. "I think," said Rowdy grimly, "that we've just made a bad mistake, old hoss. That isn't the flour sack boys outside. It's the law."

5

CATASTROPHE KATE

Although Dryfooting's claims to fame would not have filled a fat book, the town had one unique distinction at least, for Dryfooting possessed a female sheriff. Her name was Kate McCandless, but she was known as Catastrophe Kate, the sobriquet deriving from a series of marital misadventures which had indicated to even the most unobservant that marrying up with Kate was sheer catastrophe. Five neat headboards on Cemetery Hill marked the resting places of five sturdy souls who'd faced a parson with Kate. These men had died natural deaths—natural by the standards of Dryfooting—but the headboards made a mute reminder that nuptials with Kate were equivalent to getting measured for a pine box. On Leap Year's Day, the eligible males of Dryfooting usually scurried to the badlands until long after sundown. For Kate, undaunted by being five times widowed, was perennially in the market for a man.

The latest of her husbands, Curly McCandless—God rest his old bald head!—had been sheriff at the time of his demise, although he was not snatched to the hereafter in strict line of duty. Smelling smoke in the vicinity of the Tarantula Saloon, he had burst through the batwings and shouted, "Fire!" Somebody did. He left Kate a sturdy little house on the town's outskirts, a few hundred dollars in the bank, and his unfinished tenure of office. There'd been no deputy under Curly McCandless, so Kate had helped herself to the star until election time and proved herself so qualified in the interim that the citizenry had unanimously and chivalrously nominated her and swept her back into office. Now Kate was in the midst of her second qualified term.

All of which indicated that Catastrophe Kate was a considerable hunk of woman, and she was. Her weight was a consistent two hundred and twenty-five pounds, and she was broad of beam and broad of face. Her hair, a tangle of rusty gray, was kept cut short; she wore men's clothing and sat her saddle clothespin style, and she even smoked a cigar on occasion. She always had a few boxed left over after campaign time, and she saw no sense in throwing them away. She could buffalo a recalcitrant cowboy as neatly as most women could turn out a lemon pie. She was as good a sheriff as Dryfooting had ever had, and the office was likely hers as long as she wanted it.

Such was the formidable specimen of humanity who was on hand to greet Rowdy Dow and Stumpy Grampis at high noon of their second day in Dryfooting, when that precious pair awoke from much-needed sleep to find themselves stretched upon a hard cot in a cell in Dryfooting's jail. Catastrophe Kate stood in the cell corridor, frowning through the barred door. Rowdy, blinking himself awake, took one look and instantly recalled the events of the night before. This same gargantuan sight had greeted him when he'd opened their hotel door after Stumpy had put a bullet through it.

Catastrophe Kate had charged inside last night, a gun in her huge fist, and disarmed the partners who'd stood stunned at the sight of her. Then she'd hoisted the burlap-wrapped saddle under one arm, herded her prisoners out into a hallway filled with excited, questioning guests of the Seraglio, and escorted the partners to the jail. Rowdy had done a lot of protesting and made an incoherent attempt at explaining why the law had been greeted by a bullet. But Catastrophe Kate had not been in a mood to bend an attentive ear.

"It's too late of night to be jawing," she'd announced stonily. "Off to jail you go. You can wag your tongue tomorrow."

And now tomorrow had come, and the law had presented herself with the same unswerving truculence of the night before. Stumpy who'd been led to the calaboose dazedly muttering, "A female sheriff—! A female sheriff—!" was now awake and muttering the same thing all over again, but Catastrophe Kate was paying no attention to him. "Time the two of you were up," she said sternly. "What do you think this is? A rest camp for busted-down outlaws?"

Rowdy grinned. "Don't you reckon you'd better tell us just why we're jugged?"

"Shut up!" said Kate. She dug into a pocket and produced a reward dodger and held it to their view. It featured a blemished likeness of Rowdy in which a stiff derby hat rested upon his ears and an untidy cigar angled from his mouth—a picture cut from a group photograph Rowdy had been foolish enough to allow to be taken.

"It's you, ain't it?" Catastrophe Kate demanded. "The

description fits, anyway. Weight: one hundred and seventy pounds. Height: five feet eleven. Eyes: hazel. Hair: black and inclined to curl. You're the same Rowdy Dow, and no use pretending different. The one the governor was crazy enough to pardon just because you saved a bunch of folks. From a forest fire, wasn't it?"

"I blew it out, ma'am," Rowdy said politely.

"None of your lip, now! Your boldness won't get you any farther than it did last night. Just as soon as that poor girl got into town at midnight and came to me with her story of being robbed by outlaws, I began checking to see if any suspicious strangers had arrived. I hadn't been in town myself until late evening. I thought your names were familiar the minute I spied them on the Seraglio's register. The nerve of you, signing up under your own names! And when I got Bert Beecham awake and asked about you, he admitted you'd been lugging a burlap-wrapped saddle when you'd come to the hotel. Sure enough, that saddle was in your room when I arrested you —the very saddle the girl had described. But the thing that really clinches your case is that you tried to shoot me when I came to do my duty. Being pardoned for your past sins doesn't excuse what you've done lately, Rowdy Dow."

"I tried to tell you last night," Rowdy said patiently, "that we were protecting that saddle until we could hand it back to its owners. Do you blame us for being edgy when you came to our door? Somebody had tried to crawl through our window just an hour before."

Catastrophe Kate snorted. "So you said last night. Do you think I believe that hog-wash? How come the whole hotel slept through the ruckus you mentioned? Hooded men crawling up ladders and raising hell in general, and nobody misses a wink!"

"They didn't bring a brass band along!" Rowdy declared with a show of heat. "Where's that sharp-shooting girl who owned the saddle? I take it she's in town since she's the one who put you on our trail last night. Maybe what I say will make sense to her. She's seen that flour sack bunch in action."

"She's waiting in my office," Catastrophe Kate said. "Her and her grandfather, Mr. Faust. I asked them to come and identify you as the man she saw toting off her saddle out in the badlands. It will go easier with you, Dow, if you'll tell where the rest of your gang is hiding. Out in the badlands?"

"Fetch the girl," Rowdy said wearily.

Catastrophe Kate had merely to raise her voice. The corridor upon which the cells abutted had a door at its far end, and this door, Rowdy remembered, gave into the sheriff's office which faced upon the street. Kate's strident summons brought two people into the corridor, the buckskin-clad girl, and the man in black broadcloth whom Rowdy had last seen out in the badlands. These two came to a stand before the cell, and Catastrophe Kate pointed an accusing finger at Rowdy. "Is this the man, Miss Bolton?" she demanded.

Nan Bolton, modestly billed as the greatest sharpshooter of all time, was kind to the eye when viewed close up. Her buckskin garb clung intimately to a curvaceous body, and her face was the kind a man saw in lonely campfires. There was a hint of stubbornness in chin and mouth, but her eyes, blue and long-lashed, were tolerant. She studied Rowdy for a moment and said, "I can't be sure. He was far up on the rimrock when he appeared with the saddle in his arms, and I'm afraid I was too angry to be seeing straight. And I only had a glimpse of him."

Nathaniel Faust stirred. A man seamed of face but sharp of eye, he made a fine figure in black, and his spine was remarkably straight for a man of his obvious years.

Silvery hair grew long at the nape of his neck, and he had a dignity that was more than professional. But it was his hands that held Rowdy's eye, for they were the hands of an artist, long and slender and eloquent of movement. He gestured now, turning his palms upward, and Rowdy half expected to see a rabbit appear from nowhere. "I suggest this entire matter be dropped," Faust said. "We've recovered our saddle, and the damage to our coach was slight. The evidence is far too flimsy to warrant our pressing charges against these men."

"Now just a minute," Rowdy interjected. "It doesn't happen to be as simple as all that. This female sheriff has got us charged with shooting a hole in her hat. Whether we were justified depends on whether we've been telling a straight story. Sure, we were out there on the rimrock. We saw your coach attacked by those hooded galoots, but we were too far away to help. But we did manage to get the saddle away from the one who rode off with it. We'd have given it back to you then, but the girl, here, was too fancy with her rifle. We toted the saddle to town, aiming to turn it over to the sheriff. We even asked the hotel man where we could find the law. He said the sheriff was out looking for rustlers who'd been running off Winged-H stock. But the fact that we asked should prove that our intentions were honest."

Catastrophe Kate took on a stubborn look. "It only proves that you were interested in the whereabouts of the law," she countered. "Once you heard I was out of town, you figgered it was safe to spend a night in a comfortable bed."

Rowdy kept a tight hold on his temper. "The flour sack boys found out we were in town and had the saddle with us," he went on patiently. "They made a try at getting it last night—and failed. We figured they'd try again. When somebody rattled our doorknob, we jumped to conclusions. They happened to be the wrong conclusions."

Nathaniel Faust appraised him shrewdly and said, "One question, sir: do you have any idea who those hooded men are?"

"Maybe yes, maybe no," Rowdy said guardedly. "I seem to have dealt myself into this game whether I like it or not. It's got so personal that I aim to play it out. But I'm keeping a few cards tight against my vest. Telling who I think is the head of those hooded men wouldn't get me out of this pokey. That jasper would just have a big fat lie all ready to prove he couldn't have been putting a ladder up to our window last night. But how about your telling *me* something? Just what makes that saddle so valuable."

Faust smiled. "It is only valuable to one man," he said. "That man isn't you, Mr. Dow. You'll have to excuse me for not being more explicit than that."

Nan Bolton said, "We'll have to be going now, Grandfather. We've a performance to make in this town tonight, remember." Her blue eyes flicked to Rowdy. "If you were one of those hooded men, you'll probably try to lay your hands on the saddle again," she said. "Yesterday I was merely shooting to keep those men at a distance. The next time, I'll be shooting to kill. But perhaps your story is true and you were trying to do me a service. In that case, I'm grateful. You can remember whichever of my remarks *really* applies to you, and forget the other. Do I make myself clear."

"Perfectly," Rowdy said and took on an inspired look. "But it happens that I can *prove* that I aimed to turn the saddle over to you!"

Nan's eyes softened. "So? Then I'm sorry for half of what I just said. What is this proof, Mr. Dow?"

"It's so simple that I overlooked it until just now. A fellow wearing a checkered shirt, a wild horse hunter call-

ing himself the Rimrock Kid, gave you a hand in that
fracas out in the badlands yesterday. Right? The Kid came
to town last night, and I happened to be able to help save
his hide for him. We talked afterward, and I told him I
was the galoot who'd appeared on the rimrock with the
saddle. Likewise I told him that you were to get your
saddle back whenever you reached town. How does that
stack up?"

The girl said, "Yes, the Rimrock Kid proved himself to
be a friend. He saw strangers in trouble and risked his life
to come to our aid. I see your point. You wouldn't have
told *him* you had the saddle unless you truly meant to
return it. If *he* tells me that what you've just said is true, I
can see no reason why you should be kept jailed."

Rowdy shot a triumphant glance at Catastrophe Kate.
"Rattle your keys, lady," he said. "The Rimrock Kid will
back me up till my belly caves in."

"The Kid doesn't happen to be in town," the sheriff
snapped. "Likely he's gone back to his camp out in the
badlands. It might be a week before he rides in again. I've
got more to do, mister, than chouse out witnesses who'll
probably make a liar out of you once they're hazed to
town."

"Then turn me loose and I'll fetch him," Rowdy said.

"You'd hit the grit for Canada instead," Kate retorted.
"Once an outlaw, always an outlaw. That's what my late
husband told me."

"You can keep Stumpy here as hostage," Rowdy suggested. "If I don't show back with the Kid, you'll still have
a prisoner. You don't reckon I'd leave Stumpy to rot here,
do you?"

Stumpy, silent all this while, began a wild protest, but
Catastrophe Kate was looking at the little man now, looking at him as though she were seeing him for the first
time. It had been mighty dark last night. Her broad face

softened with a smile. "What do *you* think of the proposition, Mr. Grampis?" she asked.

"*Mister* Grampis—" Rowdy ejaculated.

"I'll take a chance on releasing this partner of yours if it's O.K. with you, Mr. Grampis," Catastrophe Kate went on. "I searched my files plumb to the bottom this morning, and there's no reward dodger, new or old, with your name and description. Looks to me like you're an honest man led astray by bad influence."

Now it was an exceedingly sore spot with Stumpy that the law had never publicized him by posting his picture on barns and fences. An old-timer who'd been in turn a freighter, prospector and cowhand, he'd ridden beyond the law on more than one occasion and thus had felt it necessary, when a harassed governor had pardoned Rowdy Dow, to scrawl his own name into the document that had made his partner a free man. Stumpy had worked hard at being a curly and uncombed wolf of ill repute, and all to no avail. So he said sourly, "You've got it the wrong end which-to. I'm the bad one o' the pair of us. It was *me* put that bullet through the door last night!"

Catastrophe Kate scowled fiercely at Rowdy. "So you let him handle the gun and run the risk," she snapped. "A fine thing! Encouraging a kindly old man to get into trouble! Why, one look at Mr. Grampis would convince anybody that he's honest plumb through! You ought to be ashamed of yourself, Dow!"

Rowdy said, "Are you letting me fetch in the Rimrock Kid?"

"Turn him loose," Stumpy muttered gloomily. "I'll set here in this pokey meanwhile. Turn him loose before you start getting *me* to believe them things you're saying. But I don't recollect that Rowdy was twisting my arm last night. Seems like that shooting was my own idee."

Nan Bolton and her grandfather were already heading

up the corridor toward the office. Catastrophe Kate unhooked a ring of keys from her belt, selected one and fitted it into the cell door. As she swung the door wide, allowing Rowdy to step outside, she said, "You'd better get back as quick as you can. I'm not sure this is something I ought to be doing. If you don't show back I'll have no choice but to keep Mr. Grampis locked up, in spite of any personal feelings about the matter. Remember that."

"He eats like a horse," Rowdy said. "This is going to cost the county plenty."

Behind, in the cell in which he was now the lone occupant, Stumpy's voice rose to a wail. "I'm countin' on you, Rowdy," he cried. "I'm countin' on you mighty hard. Something tells me I'm a damfool for being part and parcel to any such a deal. I ain't liking this pokey. Not a bit."

RIDDLE IN RIME

Rowdy rode out of Dryfooting less than an hour later, a restaurant meal warming his in'ards, a crude map of the badlands tucked in his pocket, and his gun rubbing at his hip. Catastrophe Kate had supplied the map; it showed various landmarks by which a man might judge his whereabouts, and it indicated the location of such ranches as were strewn through the rocky country. An X marked the spot where the Rimrock Kid, that wandering chouser of wild horses, was most likely to be found. The map would expedite Rowdy's search, and he was grateful for it. Also, he was grateful for his gun. Dryfooting's sheriff had been reluctant about returning it to him; she'd argued that freeing an outlaw was a bad enough business but that arming one was worse.

"Supposing a snake takes a bite at me?" Rowdy had countered.

He'd won his point, and he wasted little time putting Dryfooting behind him. But first he'd taken a careful ride the length of the street, studying such saddlers as stood dispiritedly at saloon hitchrails, and he hadn't known whether to be pleased or chagrined at not finding any mounts bearing the Winged-H brand. Jake Kelhorn and his cohorts had obviously shaken the dust of Dryfooting, which might mean that they were on the trail ahead. Kelhorn, Rowdy judged, would be nursing a monstrous anger today. The fellow would be plumb frustrated.

And so, with the town lost from view and each plodding step of his horse taking him deeper into a welter of serrated ridges and misshapen hillocks, Rowdy rode warily, mindful that the badlands were just naturally built for bush-whacking. Today this country cast a depressing spell upon him; the gaunt, brown towers, the dark, red walls of stone, the squat and ugly boulders had become things of menace rather than of beauty. He tried shaking this feeling by finding familiar shapes in the wind-carved sandstone, and he spied church spires and the kneeling figures of cloaked worshipers, and an upthrust rock shaped exactly like Stumpy's nose. He chuckled then, remembering Stumpy's forlorn look when he'd left his partner. Stumpy was in no danger. Catastrophe Kate McCandless had most definitely taken a shine to Stumpy Grampis.

The afternoon was half gone and Rowdy had looked many times at his crude map when he came upon the camp of the Rimrock Kid. A huge escarpment, standing lonely in a stretch of desolation, shadowed a small tent, a crude corral, and a litter of gear, but there was nobody about. Yet the sign said that the Kid had built a breakfast fire this very morning. Rowdy glanced up at the huge rock in whose shelter he stood. It was all of a hundred and fifty feet long and half as wide, and it stood naked in a wide emptiness. A man could scale it, Rowdy judged upon close examination, and he suspected that its flattish summit would give a considerable view of country. Perhaps the Kid used this as a lookout station, spotting wild horse herds. Perhaps he was aloft at the moment. Cupping his hands to his mouth, Rowdy called: "Kid! Hey, Kid!"

Echoes came back to him, some so startlingly close as to make him jump, some distant and eerie and taunting. Multiple voices cried, *"Kid! Hey, Kid!"* until the sound dwindled and was lost in an immensity of shuddering silence.

A helluva country, Rowdy decided.

He got out the map again and had a look at it, hoping that Catastrophe Kate had indicated some nearby canyons where the Kid might be building horse traps. Nothing of the sort was shown, but Rowdy, whose only interest in the map heretofore had been to find this camp, noted now that the Winged-H ranch was not far distant, lying to the northwest of here. Rowdy fished a stub of pencil from one pocket, and an old tally book from another. Tearing a page from the tally book, he scribbled a brief note to the Kid, requesting that he report to the sheriff as soon as possible. "Am heading for the Winged-H," Rowdy added on impulse and signed his name. The note weighted down before the tent by a rock, Rowdy climbed into his saddle and reined toward Caleb Hackett's ranch.

He found the place within an hour, but in the scanty miles between the Kid's camp and Hackett's domain, the country underwent a subtle change. Those white sandstone monstrosities still cluttered the land, but here was water—Rowdy thrice had to ford a thin and sinuous creek that clamored lustily across the terrain—and here was feed. The dark, rich loam of the neighboring plains put a carpet upon the barren rock, and grass grew bountifully, and sleek cattle grazed upon it. These bore the Winged-H brand, and Rowdy wasn't surprised to come shortly upon the ranch buildings.

They lay in an open space and upon a slight rise of land, and there was a two-storied frame ranch house with a gallery fronting it, a barn, a bunkhouse and corrals, a windmill and tank, and a scattering of small buildings. The yard before the ranch house was fenced, and, just inside the fence, rose two poles surmounted by a cross-arm from which was suspended a huge brass bell with a pull-rope. Horses stomped in the corrals, and smoke rose lazily from the ranch house chimney, but there were no figures moving from bunkhouse to barn, and the place had an air of desertion. But, drawing nearer, Rowdy detected a figure upon the gallery steps, and when he dismounted before the gate, looping the reins over a post, he saw that the man was a diminutive Mexican, sleepy-looking and wicked of eye.

"Caleb Hackett live here?" Rowdy inquired.

"*Si.*"

"I'd like a word with him. In fact I'd like a whole flock of words with him."

The Mexican's glance lazily and insolently measured Rowdy, drifting from the cased gun downward to his benchmade boots and back up to his deceptive choir boy face. "Senor Hackett, he ees one damn' seeck hombre," said the Mexican. "I, Pablo Diablo, have the instructions to see that he ees not disturbed. *Vamos.*"

"Where's the rest of the crew of this spread?"

Pablo Diablo shrugged. "The segundo, Jake Kelhorn, has take the boys for a ride. Soon they return, hombre. They are *mucho malo,* thees Winged-H *vaqueros.* But, by the patron saint of Guadeloupe, there is none so tough as myself, Pablo Diablo. *Vamos,* gringo, before I cut out your gizzard just to see what makes heem teeck."

"Yeah?" said Rowdy—and went into action.

Within Rowdy Dow there'd been a rankling animosity across the miles, a feeling so latent as to be hardly recognizable. If he'd stopped to analyze it he might have discovered that Catastrophe Kate had put an itch in his knuckles. Masculinity had taken a beating from Dryfooting's sheriff last night and today, leaving Rowdy with a nameless urge to avenge his sex—and no means by which to do it. This Winged-H man provided an opportunity for Rowdy to re-establish his self-respect. Not that Rowdy had any particular animosity toward Mexicans. He'd taken more than one *pasear* beyond the brimstone border and had found the dusky sons of manana land to his liking. But this Pablo Diablo—what a name!—was the exception that proved the rule. Rowdy had engendered a vast distaste for him with little effort.

So now he leaped for Pablo Diablo, leaped and got a hold on the man and hauled him from the gallery steps. One of Pablo's hands darted to the sash wound around his middle, and a wicked-looking blade gleamed in the sunlight. Rowdy twisted the knife away and sent it spinning. Then he hoisted Pablo aloft, holding him by the nape of the neck and the crotch of his pants, and, glancing around, Rowdy spied a rain barrel which stood beneath a water spout at one corner of the gallery. Pablo Diablo fitted nicely into the barrel, head down. Fortunately the barrel had heretofore been empty. With Pablo's legs flailing wildly and muffled imprecations in the name of the patron saint of Guadeloupe pouring from the barrel, Rowdy dusted his hands, mounted the gallery steps, and strode boldly into the house.

The door gave into a wide hallway which was flanked by other doors. At the far end of the hall a stairs climbed upward. Rowdy raised his voice and called: "Hackett! Caleb Hackett!" and an answer came drifting downward from the region of the stairs. "Up here," it said, and Rowdy mounted the stairs, found another hallway with flanking doors, and one of these was open.

Framing himself in the doorway, Rowdy looked into a spacious bedroom which was furnished with Spartan simplicity and centered by a bed big enough to accommodate a horse. Lost in the immensity of this bed was a gnarled little man with silvery, tousled hair, who sat propped against a pillow, a scattering of stockmen's journals on the bed before him. This nightgown-clad creature's face was sun-browned and lined with wrinkles, his eyes were small and sparkled with a perpetual anger, and his voice was too deep for the size of his body. He regarded Rowdy with frank disapproval.

"Who the hell are you?" the oldster demanded petulantly.

"Rowdy Dow. You're Caleb Hackett?"

"So you're Dow," Hackett said. "I saw your picture once. On a reward dodger. You don't look much like him. What in thunderation kept you? I expected you weeks ago. Don't stand there gaping, like you didn't have the sense you were born with! Come in. Come in. Damn it all, ain't there any men left with brains? Saddle-polishers and gun-dogs I can get by the dozens. Bah! Dow, you don't look like a helluva lot!"

It was Rowdy's thought that a man could truly pleasure himself by hauling Caleb Hackett out of yonder bed, finding another rain-barrel and standing the Winged-H owner on his head in it. But the obvious bridled his anger. "You're sick," he said.

"Sick! Do I look sick? Are you blind as well as stupid? Of course I'm not sick. That cedar-headed Jake Kelhorn just thinks I am. Kelhorn's my segundo. Ain't worth a Mexican *centavo* a day. Keep me so doped up with medicine I can't wiggle a finger. Pull up a chair. Where's that thieving son of Sonora, Pablo Diablo? He's supposed to stick around to wait on me. Probably asleep in the hayloft. I'll write out his time."

"Pablo Diablo," said Rowdy, "didn't want to let me in to see you. I roughed him up a little. He may be up in the hayloft by now, but he isn't sleeping. He's keeping his tail tucked between his legs while he licks his hurts."

A smile crinkled across the crusty face of Caleb Hackett, and Rowdy found his dislike for this irascible old man diminishing. Hackett said, "Good. Good enough. So you took the starch out of Pablo. Maybe you're worth the postage stamp I wasted writing a letter to you. Mind you, I'm not sure yet!"

"You're still hiring me?" Rowdy asked cautiously.

"Of course. When I hire a man, I don't fire him till he proves he couldn't pour sand out of a boot with the instructions written on the heel. Why shouldn't I be hiring you? Do you think I'm some old woman who changes her mind twenty times a day? Pull up a chair."

Rowdy obeyed, edging a chair toward the bed and seating himself. Tilting back in the chair, he raised his boots to the bed and crossed them there. He had learned one thing for sure. Jake Kelhorn had been acting on his own when he'd told Rowdy that Hackett no longer required Rowdy's services. But Rowdy had guessed as much in Dryfooting. Shaping up a cigarette, he said, "What's this about Griffen's Gold? You said you could cut me in on a share of it."

"That fetched you, eh? You ever hear tell of Griffen—Joshua Griffen? But probably you're too young to remember. Griffen came out to the Alder Gulch region. During the gold rush days of the early sixties. Struck it rich. Started back to the States with a covered wagon train, him and a bunch of other pilgrims who'd filled their pokes. Damfools got themselves ambushed by a band of marauding Sioux right here in these badlands. A massacre. But before they were wiped out, Griffen buried his gold."

"How do you know?" Rowdy inquired.

"How do I know? How do you suppose I know? Old-timers have been telling the story of Griffen's Gold for years. And looking for it. Griffen was captain of that wagon train. He kept a journal. It was almost burned up when the Sioux fired the wagons after the massacre. But not quite. Passages mention that Griffen was afraid the Indians were stalking them. Or so I've heard. Right then and there he figgered on burying the gold if the Indians got too close. For years that journal was in Dryfooting. The newspaper office used to display the thing in the window. I told Kelhorn to find out what become of it, but he's likely forgot. Can't depend on that fool for ten minutes. Not that it makes any difference. The gold ain't where Griffen buried it anyway."

"You mean it was found?"

"Found and moved by a locoed old prospector called Tennyson Tolbert. An old goat who wrote poems—bad poems. He's dead now, and I hope they buried the fool upside down! He found Griffen's gold, Dow, and he was supposed to give half of it to me. I grubstaked that ungrateful son for years. A prospector is supposed to give half of what he finds to the man who grubstaked him. And Tennyson Tolbert found gold—Griffen's Gold. Hoist up the mattress and reach under it. Down at the far end. You'll find a letter."

Rowdy obeyed, groping until his fingers touched paper. The letter was soiled and wrinkled and was addressed to Caleb Hackett, in care of the Winged-H ranch. The postmark was almost obliterated, but Rowdy managed to make out the date, some three months past, and saw that the missive had been mailed from Hamilton, Montana.

Hamilton, Rowdy recalled, was in the Bitterroot Valley in the western part of the state.

"Look inside," Hackett urged. "It's from Tolbert. Tried all these years to cheat me. His conscience got too much for him when he knew he was dying. Afraid old St. Pete would shake him down at the gate and find him burdened with more sins than ten men could carry. Look inside."

Rowdy shook out the letter. It read:

Dear Caleb:

I've been here in the Bitterroot for close to five years and have been ailing all the time. Lung trouble, the doctor says. Now he tells me I haven't got very long to live. If there's anything that needs squaring up, he says, I'd better take care of it.

Hang onto your chair, you hard-fisted old hellion. I found Griffen's Gold before I left the badlands. Yes, I know you are entitled to half of it, but maybe I'd have given it to you, and maybe I wouldn't. You grubstaked me, sure, but you were mighty mean about it, and it rankles me to hand anything back to you. And now you'll be getting it all because I won't be alive to lay hold of my own half. I found the gold and buried it again and have been hoping these five years to get back to it.

I'm going to make it tough for you. I'm going to make you work for it, just like I worked all those years, starving out there in those rocks and hoping to strike it rich. I'm enclosing a little poem for you. You always laughed at my poems, remember? I don't think you'll laugh at this one. It tells you how to find Griffen's Gold. But you'll have to rack your old brain, and I hope it gives you a headache that'll last the rest of your life.

Even now I think I'm a blasted fool to be putting anything in your hands. But I'm really doing it for the sake of Esmerelda—God rest her soul. She was always mighty kind to me, and she was your flesh and blood, even though she had no reason to be proud of it.

See you in hell!

                                        Tennyson Tolbert

Rowdy lifted his eyes. "Who was Esmerelda?" he asked.

"My daughter!" Hackett snapped. "She run off twenty years ago with a jigger who was so worthless I wouldn't have wasted a chunk of lead on him. That damn' Tennyson Tolbert encouraged her to do it, too. Esmerelda's the one who first got me to grubstake Tolbert. And that's the thanks I got for it!"

Rowdy had been studying this pepper-skinned, fiery-tongued oldster, and Rowdy's first dislike had given way to a baffled feeling of being unable to peg this man properly. This in turn had been tempered by a tolerance growing from the feeling that Hackett's health accounted for his vitriolic attitude. Now Rowdy sensed a deeper reason for what Caleb Hackett was. The man had pride in him, and stubbornness too, and a great bitterness that had blossomed across many years. Now Rowdy thought he knew why. The key was in the man's reference to the daughter who'd apparently deserted him. That incident of long ago had left its mark on Caleb Hackett. Bend the trunk of a tree ever so slightly and it grows crooked. And now Rowdy said softly, "She's dead?"

"Many years," Hackett replied, and his own voice turned soft.

But only for a moment. "I'm hiring you, Dow, because I think you've got the brains to unravel the mess that Tennyson Tolbert put in my hands. Or so I'm hoping. I've read about you in the papers and you stack up good in print. Jake Kelhorn thinks otherwise. Said I was crazy the

day I sent him to town to post that letter to you. I'm a
hard man to get along with, but I'm a just man, and you'll
get a fair share of the gold if you can make any sense out
of what Tolbert sent me. Take a look at it and tell me if
you want the job."

The envelope had contained a second sheet. Rowdy
separated it from the letter and had a look at it. Scrawled
in the now-familiar fist of Tennyson Tolbert was a poem, a
poem that had Rowdy's senses reeling before he was half
through it. This was the way it read:

"If the Devil's Saddle's too hot for your pants
    When the April sun is hell,
Injun down from that kak and bend your old back,
    When you hear your own supper bell;
Just keep to the shade that the saddlehorn's made,
    And don't be afraid to sweat;
There's no easy way to get rich in a day,
    And you'll earn all the gold that you'll get!"

7

CANYON TRAP

Very slowly Rowdy folded Tennyson Tolbert's letter and
poem and replaced them in the envelope. A fine hodge-
podge this had turned out to be! A queer prospector
who'd searched the badlands for gold and found it—the
dust that other men had panned and sluiced, dust that had
been buried when the Sioux had descended upon a wagon
train long ago . . . This same prospector reburying the
gold, then drifting to Hamilton to die of a lung ailment
. . . A cryptic letter coming to Caleb Hackett who'd
grubstaked Tennyson Tolbert at the insistence of a daugh-

ter, Esmerelda Hackett, who'd long ago left her cantankerous father . . . a nonsense poem with a reference to the devil's saddle, a poem which was supposed to point the way to where Tennyson Tolbert had re-hidden Captain Joshua Griffen's long-sought gold . . . These were the ingredients from which a mystery was made.

Yet some things were now clear which had been fathomless before. An old trouper, Nathaniel Faust, and his granddaughter, Nan Bolton, were threading through this country in a fancy stagecoach and putting on a performance in various towns—a performance which included an act called *The Devil's Saddle*. They carried a saddle with them and made no secret of it. Hooded horsemen had descended upon them outside Dryfooting and wrested that saddle away from them. Those horsemen had been Winged-H riders, even though they'd ridden unbranded horses. One had worn a broken spur, and Rowdy had recognized that same spur on Jake Kelhorn in the Seraglio early last evening. Kelhorn and his crew had changed horses somewhere in the badlands, ridden on into town, and, in due time, Kelhorn had approached Rowdy with the spurious word that Caleb Hackett no longer hungered for Rowdy's services. Moreover, Kelhorn had displayed an interest in the saddle and tried to buy it. Later there'd been that attempt to reach the room by night, an attempt made by those same hooded men.

Plainly, Jake Kelhorn was playing a game of his own. Kelhorn had known of the letter Caleb Hackett had received from Tennyson Tolbert—the letter Rowdy now held in his hand. Kelhorn had also known of Hackett's intention to hire Rowdy Dow to help crack the riddle in rime which Tolbert had enclosed. Kelhorn had tried to discourage that, and, failing, had attempted a hoax by telling Rowdy that he was no longer needed. Kelhorn, in the meantime, had been after the Devil's Saddle himself.

Those posters had doubtless been before the Dryfooting Opera House a couple of weeks, and they had caught Kelhorn's eye. The man had probably questioned the theater manager, learned where Faust was then performing, and determined the approximate time when the show people would reach the badlands. Whereupon Kelhorn had lain in wait.

Such was the way Rowdy saw it, but the voice of Caleb Hackett broke in jarringly upon his meditation. "Well?" the Winged-H owner rasped. "Fallen asleep on your feet? Or are you trying to stare a hole through the wall? What do you make of it? Speak up!"

Rowdy grinned. In this brief interview with Hackett he'd grown used to the oldster's barbed tongue and it no longer aroused him to anger. The question in Rowdy's mind was how much of the truth he dared tell Hackett. The man was virtually a prisoner here, and the man was also blind to this fact and to the true nature of Jake Kelhorn. Hackett had ranted about Kelhorn, much as he ranted about everyone, but none of his remarks had indicated that he distrusted his foreman. Even Pablo Diablo, stationed here by Kelhorn to see that no one reached Hackett, was, in the oldster's eyes, a servant provided for his comfort. No, Caleb Hackett was definitely blind to the true state of affairs.

Whereupon Rowdy elected to hold certain cards close to his vest for the time being. Jake Kelhorn was making sure his boss stayed bedded down so that Caleb Hackett wouldn't be riding to Dryfooting where the oldster might accidentally scan the billboards before the opera house. Perhaps Kelhorn might even know more than he was telling about the disappearing Winged-H cattle whose theft was being laid to the Rimrock Kid. That could be another reason why Kelhorn was making sure his boss didn't know what was happening on his own ranch. But Kelhorn, at the pace he was traveling, was shortly going to tangle his own twine. In the meantime, as Rowdy saw it, there was no sense in making accusations against the foreman, none of which could be really proved.

He dropped his glance to Hackett. "I never could make any sense out of poetry," Rowdy said. "But this is even crazier than that fellow Shakespeare's stuff. It doesn't give us much to work on."

"I've puzzled over it, Dow. So has Jake. Anyway you look at it, the thing starts out with some gabble about a devil's saddle. You've covered a lot of country. Ever hear tell of such a fool thing?"

"Maybe. Supposing I have?"

Hackett reared upright in bed. "Then for Pete's sake show your cards! I've offered you a cut. I'll make it a dime out of every dollar the gold fetches. I've got to get it. I've got to get it to fool Tennyson Tolbert, if for no other reason. I'll bet if you walked across his grave today, you'd hear him chuckling. Chuckling because he's got me near crazy with his fool riddle. Yes, he's dead. I wrote to Hamilton and they told me he was dead and buried. Quit poking a stick into me, Dow. If you've ever heard of the Devil's Saddle, tell me about it!"

"I know a man who owns a saddle he calls by that name," Rowdy said slowly. "He told me—and not long ago—that the saddle was valuable to only one man. I reckon he meant you. How much he really knows, I can't be sure. Would you be willing to do business with him— cut him in on another ten percent, say, of the gold in exchange for the saddle?"

"Ten percent to you!" Hackett howled. "Ten percent to this other jigger! I'll end up with nothing, if I don't watch out!"

Rowdy's anger rose in spite of himself. "You old goat!" he snapped. "Whatever you're getting out of this is more than you deserve. You grubstaked Tolbert, sure. But only because your daughter got you to do it. Tolbert spent years out in the badlands, wandering around under a hot sun. When he found Griffen's Gold, he buried it again, not intending to give you half of it. Can't say that I blame him. But when he found himself dying, he decided to give you a chance at it. He's making your work tough for you, but not nearly as tough, probably, as it was for him to find that gold in the first place. You figure on lying in this bed and hiring somebody else to do what you haven't got the brains to do. You want me to get that gold and lay it in your lap. And now you're hollering because you won't get a full one hundred percent. To hell with you!"

He expected his anger to be paled by a greater anger on the part of Caleb Hackett. He expected that his outburst would arouse Hackett to a wild fury and that the air would be full of vituperation and profanity. Instead, Hackett's seamed face broke into a broad grin. "You'll do, Dow," he said admiringly. "You'll do. If you really know somebody who's got the Devil's Saddle, go dicker with him. Any deal you make will be O.K. by me. You're my agent from here on out. I'll tie no strings on you."

Rowdy grinned too, his anger gone. "How do you know whether I'll ever show back once I lay my hands on that gold, Hackett?"

"You'll show back," Hackett said. "Did you think I was buying a pig in a poke when I sent for you? Looked your record up from one end to the other. Outside the law and in. Money never meant a hoot to you. It was the adventure you wanted. You play square. I know that. I'm trusting you."

And that, Rowdy had to concede, was as effective a way of tying a man's hands as any. There was a native shrewdness to this Caleb Hackett that made him nobody's fool.

Rowdy extended his hand. "It's a deal," he said. "I'll be riding now. I'll see you again when I've something to report."

They shook hands, and Rowdy moved toward the doorway. He had good reason for wanting to be away from this ranch before Jake Kelhorn and the crew returned from wherever they were keeping themselves, but, pausing in the doorway, he took time to say: "Was I you, Hackett, I'd pour such medicine as was fetched to me out of the window. No need to tell Kelhorn. If he thinks you're sick, you might as well humor him for a spell."

"Good idea," Hackett agreed.

A moment later Rowdy was descending the stairs to the lower floor of this big ranch house. When he came out upon the gallery, the Winged-H still had its air of desertion, and there was no sign of that *malo hombre,* the toughest of them all, Pablo Diablo. The overturned rain barrel, empty of Mexicans, was eloquent of the means by which Pablo had extricated himself. Rowdy grinned. His horse still stood at the gate. He swung up into the saddle and headed toward Dryfooting, but not by the most direct route. He was angling to where the Rimrock Kid had his camp; there was the possibility that the Kid had since showed up, in which case the two of them could ride to town together. Whereupon they would peel the Dryfooting pokey off one Stumpy Grampis.

The thought of Stumpy widened Rowdy's grin. Shortly Stumpy would learn that Rowdy Dow had been right in his surmise about Jake Kelhorn, and Stumpy would likewise learn that they were not heading back to the Little Belts but were instead assigned to the job that had originally brought them here. Stumpy would show a great unenthusiasm and would doubtless berate Rowdy and brand him as an unmitigated, adventurous fool. But

Stumpy would be secretly pleased. Stumpy, for all his talk, liked to be up to his hairy ears in wild goings-on.

From a high crest Rowdy had a view of the open land below, and here he could see that gigantic upthrust of rock that shadowed the Kid's camp. It seemed as though a man could almost reach out and touch that bleak and lonely sentinel of the badlands, but, between Rowdy and the rock was a stretch of canyon country, broken and tangled. He dipped down into these canyons and began feeling his way along in the general direction of his destination, and he shortly began to wonder if emulating the crow was such a wise practice since he was not possessed of wings. Better, perhaps, to retrace his steps and journey from the Winged-H to the Kid's camp by the route he'd come, a much flatter traverse. Then he heard the hoofbeats. Hauling his mount to a stand, Rowdy listened intently. At least a half-dozen riders were here in these rocks, and he judged that they were moving his way.

This was still the Winged-H's domain, and that gave Rowdy a good idea of whom he was likely to find out here. He had no desire to meet Jake Kelhorn at this moment; Kelhorn would be mighty angry over what had happened last night when a ladder had been fetched to the Seraglio, and Kelhorn might make so bold as to reveal his anger, even though it meant implicating himself in the attempt at stealing the saddle. Rowdy glanced hastily around. Other canyons led off from this one, and it behooved Rowdy to make himself scarce. But suddenly it was too late.

The oncoming horsemen had rounded a bend. Big in the saddle was Jake Kelhorn, and with him were those men who'd rigged a gun-trap in the Tarantula last night, but there was one among them who had not been present in the saloon. Pablo Diablo. The little Mexican rode at

Kelhorn's left stirrup, and it was he who first spied Rowdy and raised a shout. Instantly Rowdy was wheeling his horse and heading for cover. Pablo Diablo's presence had told him all he needed to know. Pablo had come to fetch Kelhorn and the crew, and Pablo had known where to find the Winged-H riders. And Pablo had undoubtedly brought word that a trespasser had appeared at the ranch and forced an audience with Caleb Hackett.

A fine kettle of fish! Kelhorn would now realize that Rowdy knew that Kelhorn had been misrepresenting his boss when Kelhorn had come to the Seraglio. And Kelhorn, accordingly, would no longer be maintaining the pretense of good fellowship he'd displayed in the hotel. In fact Kelhorn was already unmasking himself. A gun was in his hand, and a bullet chipped rock as Rowdy headed his horse into a rocky slot. Other Winged-H riders, taking their cue from the segundo, began shooting too; they lifted their voices in wild shouts, and the echoes, multiplying this cacophony of strident sound, made a bedlam of the badlands.

Into another canyon and racing wildly along its boulder-littered length, Rowdy found himself safe for the moment from questing lead, but not for long. The Winged-H riders were behind him, and a hasty glance over his shoulder gave Rowdy a glimpse of them. They were bent low over saddlehorns and quirting hard, and the guns began barking again. Rowdy got his own gun into his hand and made it speak, but he wasted no time at aiming. He only hoped to discourage the pursuit from venturing too close, but, in the meantime, Rowdy's real intent was to outride them and lose himself.

Scant chance of that, he quickly learned. His one glance behind had shown him only four men; now, with this canyon pinching together to form a dead end, he saw two other canyons angling off from it. He turned into one of these, heard a wild and triumphant shout far behind him, and instantly turned back. Ahead, briefly outlined as they came racing between boulders, were three other Winged-H men. The outfit had split, one part maneuvering to head him off, and he'd almost blundered right into their arms. Wheeling his mount and returning to the canyon he'd just quitted, he saw the original four riders, Kelhorn among them. The four were much closer, but there was still time for Rowdy to thunder into the other angling canyon.

Rowdy was now growing desperate. He'd learned how futile would be any attempt to outmaneuver the pursuit. They knew these canyons intimately, as they'd already proved, and he could only gallop along, harried and hunted and hoping that whatever turn he might take would be the right one. But each time he made a wrong move, they gained on him. Better, he decided grimly, to get afoot and into the rocks and make a stand somewhere. With a boulder to shelter him he could keep that whole bunch mighty busy if things settled down to a siege.

Yet that would hardly be wise strategy either. They were seven, and they were mighty near their home ranch. To fort up would merely gain him time, and time was likely to be a drug on the market, considering. They would keep him penned in the rocks and starve him out, if necessary, for two or three men could hold him at bay while the others went to the Winged-H for food and water. Night would be coming in a few hours, but that wasn't likely to prove any real advantage either. They would be able to spread out and keep him from making an escape, even with darkness to cover him.

Thus Rowdy rode recklessly, feeling like a cornered coyote and undecided as to what to do about it. Now he was deep into the canyon maze with the pursuit still clinging doggedly to his heels; shortly he was hopelessly lost and knew it. These canyons had gotten so they all looked alike; it was a matter of ride wildly the length of one, dodge into any opening that provided itself, and, just as often as not, dodge back again because his move had been anticipated and riders appeared ahead of him as well as behind him. They'd spun a fine web, and with his horse heaving beneath him, he realized that they were drawing that web even tighter.

But still there was nothing to do but ride—ride and be thankful that unsteady saddles made for poor shooting. He'd long since given up wasting lead himself; it was better to keep his eyes ahead and a firm hand on the reins. This thought was in him when he dodged into one more canyon, and the instant its walls reared above him, he realized that he'd not been in this one before, and he also realized that he'd made a mistake. This was a box canyon with precipitous walls on all sides and a wild litter of boulders strewn upon its floor. There was no escape from it, and in the moment that an awareness of this burst upon him, he knew that he'd been deliberately herded here.

Once again he wheeled his horse. His only hope was to get back out of here before the pursuit reached the entrance, but even as he brought his jaded mount around, he knew he was too late. Riders were pouring through the entrance, their guns out and blazing, and Rowdy instinctively swerved sidewards in the saddle as a bullet breathed hotly past his cheek. This was his undoing. The horse was pivoting as he made the move, and he went off balance and fell.

Kicking free of the stirrups, he saw the swarthy face of Jake Kelhorn as the Winged-H foreman bore down upon him. He saw the grinning triumph in that face, and then Rowdy was landing upon the rocky ground. His head struck against a hard, pointed object, a loose rock likely, and he grasped outward, trying to find something to fasten his hands upon. And that was when his senses deserted him.

8

CAME THE KID

Rowdy roused slowly. His first consciousness was of hard planking beneath him; he tried moving, wanting to ease his body, and he found then that he was tied. Most effectively. His ankles were lashed and so were his wrists, and he was lying on his side like a trussed hog, one ear to the floor. He could lift his head, and he did, but instantly regretted the action. A flock of heavy-footed hombres might have been dancing a fandango inside his skull. He shut his eyes tightly and held them this way for a long moment and then opened them again. His head still hammered, but not as hard as before.

"He's coming awake," somebody said. The voice wouldn't have assayed an ounce of sympathy.

Rowdy had a look around. Memory was returning with a rush—the memory of a canyon trap and horsemen closing in and guns barking and triumphant shouts filling the air. He was lying upon the floor of a bunkhouse, and it was obviously the Winged-H bunkhouse, for Kelhorn and his crew were here. Rowdy could glimpse the bunks along the wall and see some of the men who were perched upon them. In the center of this long, low building was a table, and beside it Jake Kelhorn was seated, his chair tilted back and his muscular legs crossed on the table top. Light filtered in through the windows. Daylight. The afternoon was nearly gone, but there was still the tag end of it left.

"Well," said Kelhorn, peering down at Rowdy who lay less than six feet from him, "how do you like it this far west?"

"I've seen it tougher," Rowdy said.

Kelhorn scowled, fingering the tiny scar on his left cheekbone thoughtfully. "So you saw the Old Man," he said.

"Sure. I'm one of the hands, Jake. Which means I owe you that hundred dollars you gave me. But likely you've already taken it out of my pocket."

"That smart talk won't get you anywhere," Kelhorn snapped. "Where's that stove-up partner of yours? And what became of the saddle?"

"Don't you know?"

"We rode out of Dryfooting this morning. Town talk had it that the show girl and her grandpappy got into town late last night. They went straight to the sheriff with a yarn about what had happened out in the badlands. Catastrophe Kate checked the Seraglio to see if any strangers were in town. Beecham told her about you two showing up lugging a wrapped saddle. The sheriff arrested you and toted you off to jail. But now you're here—which means you must have busted out. But this is what I want to know: did you manage to get the saddle when you made the break?"

"I can't talk so well when I'm all tied up like this, Jake. It chokes my tongue. Peel these ropes off me and maybe I'll loosen up."

"You stay tied!" Kelhorn roared. "And you'll talk. Shall I turn Pablo loose on you with his knife? Pablo hates your insides, Dow, and he knows a hatful of Yaqui tricks. It would be a pleasure to watch him perform."

A boot made soft movement on the planking and Pablo came within Rowdy's range of vision. He had his knife, the same one Rowdy had wrested away from him a few hours earlier, and he balanced the blade across the palm of one swarthy hand. "*Si,*" he said. "It would be the great fon working on you, *hombre*. By the patron saint of Guadeloupe, it would be *mucho* fun."

"I'd likely yell," Rowdy said. "I might yell so loud that Caleb Hackett would hear me in the ranch house. How would you explain to him why you were carving up his special agent like a Christmas turkey? Hackett wouldn't like that. And I don't think you're quite ready, Jake, to let the Old Man know that you're drawing his pay but you're really working for yourself. I haven't told him about you *yet*, Jake. You savvy what I mean? About the flour sacks?"

Kelhorn's face stiffened. "You can't prove a thing. If you could, you'd have likely told Catastrophe Kate. She had her chance this morning to come rattling her keys at us. She didn't."

Rowdy shrugged as well as a man might who was weighted down with ropes. "Maybe I haven't got proof," he admitted. "Not the kind that would interest Catastrophe Kate or Caleb Hackett. But we understand each other, don't we, old son? And I'm sure going to yell if that Mex starts carving his initials on my hide."

"We can gag you."

"And how will you make me talk if I've got a gag in my mouth? Jake, you're getting dull in your old age."

Kelhorn swung his feet from the table and they thudded to the floor. He came to a towering stand, took a couple of steps toward Rowdy and planted a boot in Rowdy's ribs, a hard, jarring kick. "What's become of that saddle?" Kelhorn thundered.

Rowdy's eyes narrowed and a high anger glinted in them, but he kept his temper in cheek and his voice remained affable. "Why don't you ask me polite," he said. "The saddle was returned to the show people. That's no secret. Everybody in Dryfooting will know it tonight when the old fellow puts on his magic act. Catastrophe Kate turned me loose so I could find the Rimrock Kid. That's no secret either. I had a talk with the Kid last night, after you tried sewing him up in the Tarantula. I told the Kid that we had the saddle and meant to give it back to that sharp-shooting gal. Catastrophe Kate thinks we swiped the saddle. Once the Kid tells her that we'd stated our honest and noble intentions *before* the law got hold of us, then Kate will know that we were on the level. She's keeping Stumpy in jail till I show back with the Kid."

Kelhorn stared down at him like a man bereft of his senses. "Then you *didn't* get hold of that saddle for yourself? You meant all along to give it back to the girl? Yes, I know you told me as much in the Seraglio last night, but I thought you were just throwing dust in my eyes."

"And why shouldn't I have figured on giving it back, Jake? Even if I had a crooked streak in me—and some folks will give you an argument to prove I have—I didn't know anything about the Devil's Saddle when I had it in my hands. Hackett told me the story about Tennyson Tolbert today and showed me the riddle in poetry form. That's when I first savvied why a bunch of boys with flour sacks pulled over their heads were trying so hard to get that saddle."

"That's right!" Kelhorn murmured. "I saw the letter that Hackett sent you. He mentioned Griffen's Gold, but he didn't say anything about the saddle. You couldn't have been wise until today. Not even a little bit."

"Jake," said Rowdy, "you're improving. Honest Injun, you are for a fact. Another seven years and you'll be showing the brains of a seven-year-old."

But Kelhorn was too wrapped in thought to react to the

insult. He stood silently, fingering his ragged mustache, his eyes glazed with concentration. Then he came to an awareness of his surroundings, his glance darting to his waiting crew. "We're getting places," he announced triumphantly. "We know what's become of the saddle. Now we've got to do some planning. A couple of you boys tote this jigger somewhere else. Put him out in the blacksmith shop, but make sure he's tied good and tight. I don't want him where he can hear what we've got to say."

"We don' keel him?" Pablo inquired regretfully.

"Not yet, Pablo. There's always the one chance that he's lying. Maybe he busted out of jail, and maybe he fetched the saddle with him. He's got to stay alive until we know for sure. After that you can have your fun. And when you've finished, Caleb Hackett will think that Mr. Rowdy Dow found the game too strong for his stomach and rode out. See what I mean?"

Whereupon Pablo Diablo loudly demanded of the patron saint of Guadeloupe why a man of his obvious virtues should be so shabbily treated by destiny. But he found consolation in the spoken reflection that a pleasure deferred doubled with anticipation.

A couple of Winged-H hands got a hold on Rowdy, hoisted him from the floor, lugged him out of the bunkhouse and across the yard to the blacksmith shop. Here he was dumped unceremoniously to the dirt floor, and one of the men knelt and made a careful examination of his bonds. Satisfied, the fellow grunted, and the pair departed, heading back toward the bunkhouse.

Rowdy listened until their footsteps died away and then fell to struggling with the rope. This effort served to bring the sweat out on him but was altogether futile. His eyes roved around the room, taking in the sooty, wide-throated forge, the anvil, the bench littered with scrap iron and wagon bolts and horseshoes. Nothing here to help him, and no means of laying his hands on anything that might.

The early darkness of a spring evening was crowding in on the Winged-H, and soon he heard the throaty voice of the brass bell that stood in the ranch yard before the house. A supper bell, obviously, for, within a few minutes, a man shaped up in the doorway of the blacksmith shop bearing a bucket that smelled of stew. Rowdy was untied and allowed to eat, the Winged-H hand who'd fetched the food hunkering on his heels and watching him closely the while. Thereafter Rowdy was tied again, just as firmly as before, and the Winged-H man departed. Rowdy tested the knots, just on the chance that the man might have been a mite careless. A plague on such efficiency! Panting and perspiring, Rowdy soon gave up the effort.

Shortly there was much activity. It was darker now, and even though Rowdy, by raising his head, could get a partial glimpse of the yard through the open doorway of the blacksmith shop, there was little he could see. But he heard the sounds of men at the corrals, and, interpreting these sounds, he knew that the Winged-H hands were laying ropes on fresh cayuses and saddling up. A few minutes later they had all risen to saddle; shod hoofs made plopping noises in the yard as the mounts were walked away from the ranch. Then all sound faded to nothingness.

The crew had ridden off, and apparently in the direction of Dryfooting, if Rowdy was any judge. Had all of them gone? Rowdy couldn't be sure, and he hardly knew to what use the knowledge could be put even if he possessed it with certainty. Then he remembered Caleb Hackett, bedded down in the ranch house. Would a man's voice carry from the blacksmith shop through the stout walls of the ranch house and fetch Hackett? Rowdy doubted it, but he made the try. *"Hackett!"* he called with all his strength. *"Caleb Hackett!"*

Within a very few seconds a slight form framed itself in the doorway of the blacksmith shop. It was too dark now to see the face of the man, but Rowdy recognized the soft voice. "You make the holler once more," said Pablo Diablo, "and I steeck the knife in you and twist heem hard. *Sabe?"*

He was gone as silently and as swiftly as he'd come, and Rowdy cursed his own fool luck. Of course Pablo Diablo had been left behind. Pablo's permanent job seemed to be to keep an eye on things at the ranch while Kelhorn and the others rode hither and yon on dubious business. Not a Chinaman's chance now of getting the attention of Caleb Hackett!

But this was not the greatest reason why Rowdy found no pleasure in the thought of Pablo's presence. Pablo had formed a hatred for him that would grow with each sullen reflection on the episode of this afternoon when Rowdy had overpowered the Mexican and planted him in the rain barrel. You didn't win a Mexican's undying affection by that sort of indignity. Not by a jugful. Pablo was a hard hater, and Pablo, with nothing to do but brood, would keep remembering that Rowdy was alone here and at his mercy. There'd been an avid eagerness in the man's voice. Off somewhere—not very far away, likely—Pablo would be nursing his hate. Rowdy had never supposed that he'd find himself pining for the sight of Jake Kelhorn, but he wished mightily that the foreman would return.

The night was closing in fast; out in the badlands a coyote mourned the dying day, the echoes catching the plaint and intensifying its weirdness. A half-hour passed, and Rowdy was wondering if it would be worth his while to struggle with his bonds again, and then he heard a faint, scraping sound. A man was stealing along the wall of the blacksmith shop, edging toward the doorway, and suddenly the sweat came out upon Rowdy and was cold and clammy. He fell to struggling frantically, a wild and futile effort, but it was the only kind of fight he could make, and he was sure now that he was fighting for his life. That stealthy one had almost reached the doorway. In another moment Rowdy knew that the knife of Pablo Diablo would be at his throat.

A form silhouetted itself against the last of the light—a slight form. A voice said whisperingly, "Dow? Rowdy Dow?" And Rowdy found himself near to fainting, not from terror but from relief. It was the Rimrock Kid who had come.

"Here," Rowdy said, his voice a faint croak. The darkness of the shed's interior swallowed the Kid; Rowdy made out his movements but only dimly. And then the Kid was on his knees, fumbling with the knots. Another minute or two and Rowdy was free and rubbing his wrists. He came to a stand, aided by the Kid, and stomped softly, restoring circulation, and the two of them moved out into the yard.

"Step careful," said the Kid.

Ahead, a form sprawled upon the ground. Pablo Diablo. "Tapped him with the barrel of my six-shooter," the Kid explained briefly. "This way, Dow. The corral is yonder."

"What fetched you here?" Rowdy asked, still whispering.

"Your note," said the Kid. "I found it at my camp when I came back this afternoon. When I read that you were headed for the Winged-H, I thought you must have gone loco. Couldn't see how you could expect anything but a hot-lead welcome here, seeing as how you'd stood up against Kelhorn and his boys in the Tarantula last night. So I loped this way. Here's your gun. I found it in the bunkhouse."

Rowdy strapped the belt around his waist, lifted the gun from leather and thrust it back again. "How did you know where to locate me?"

The Kid's ready grin revealed those startling white teeth of his. "Before I got to the ranch, I heard a heap of gun-thunder in the canyons. When I sighted Kelhorn and his boys, they had you hung across your own saddle like a butchered beef and were toting you in this direction. I kept 'em in sight, but kept myself covered. I've been In-juning around here ever since, waiting a chance to get close to you. There wasn't any chance until Kelhorn took the crew toward town. Then I had to stalk that kill-crazy Mex until I could get close enough to bend a gun-barrel between his horns. Your cayuse in the corral?"

They'd reached a peeled pole enclosure, and Rowdy spied his own horse inside, still saddled but with the cinch loosened. He got his hand on the mount without having to use a rope, tightened the cinch and led the animal through the gate. The Kid said, "This way. I left my horse back a piece."

They went boldly across the ranch yard and beyond it, walking a good quarter of a mile before the Kid found his mount in a cluster of rocks. When the wild horse hunter was up into saddle, Rowdy said, "*Gracias* for what you did for me tonight. We're heading for Dryfooting?"

"Dryfooting," said the Kid. "And you can do a heap more than thank me, if you like. I don't know how you fit into things hereabouts, but it's mighty plain that you're no friend of Jake Kelhorn's. That's why I'm counting on you to help me bust up his game tonight. But we'll have to ride hard. He's got a start on us."

"Meaning—?" Rowdy asked.

"Meaning that I laid out behind the bunkhouse and listened to them while I was waiting for it to get dark enough so I could prowl the place and reach you. Kelhorn and his boys aim to take in the show at the opera house tonight. And what's more, they aim to get the saddle that Nan Bolton's grandfather uses in his magic act. They don't know how they're going to get it, and they don't much care. Jake Kelhorn has turned desperate. Can I count on you, *amigo?*"

Rowdy prodded his horse to a gallop. "Let's ride," he said.

9

A HOT TIME TONIGHT

Hard riding brought Rowdy and the Rimrock Kid across the miles toward Dryfooting at a far faster pace than had marked Rowdy's trip from the town earlier today. They dissolved distance at a breathless gallop, the Kid leading the way; and the Kid traveled as the crow travels. Rowdy, a stranger to this broken country, might, out of necessity, have headed for the Kid's camp at the base of the mighty sentinel rock and then found his way back to town by attention to the stars and a constant searching for landmarks. The Kid's presence made this unnecessary. The Kid was heading as nearly directly overland as the tortured terrain permitted, and the Kid was most obviously taking the role of rescuer as seriously as the Seventh Cavalry would have done under comparable circumstances.

The way the Kid was working his quirt, it wouldn't have surprised Rowdy to have found Dryfooting surrounded by howling Indians.

Their wild riding gave them no chance to talk. Always a breeze of their own making was in their faces, flattening back the brims of their sombreros, and always the rataplan of hoofs over a rocky trail made an anarchy of sound,

enveloping them in a noisy little world of constant movement and constant clatter. A man had only his thoughts
for company on a ride like this, and Rowdy's thoughts
were upon Jake Kelhorn who was somewhere ahead, leading his crew to Dryfooting for a purpose both desperate
and ruthless.

And those were the twin traits that made Kelhorn a
formidable antagonist and one not easily circumvented.
Desperate and ruthless. A prisoner in the bunkhouse,
Rowdy had twitted Kelhorn about his stupidity, but a man
tied hand and foot had only his tongue for a weapon, and
Rowdy hadn't been underestimating Kelhorn—not even
then. From the first, the Winged-H foreman had shown a
determined intent to have his way, regardless of risk, and
against that determination Rowdy was now irrevocably
pitted. A pact with Caleb Hackett plus some personal in-
clinations on Rowdy's part made this so.

Misfortune, it seemed, only whetted Kelhorn's determination. From the time of the man's attack on the fancy
stagecoach out in the badlands, Kelhorn had made play
after play to lay his hands on that mysterious saddle, and
he wasn't quitting now. Not by a jugful. Kelhorn was going to make another play tonight, when the saddle served
as a prop in Nathaniel Faust's magic act. And Kelhorn
would likely prove himself both bold and sagacious when
the play was made. That was the man's way.

Yes, Jake Kelhorn was a foeman worthy of even
Rowdy's peculiar kind of steel, and Rowdy, glimpsing the
Rimrock Kid's dark, intent face in the starlight, wondered
if the wild horse hunter was having the same run of
thoughts. Also, he wondered exactly how much the Kid
had learned while he'd lain listening outside the
bunkhouse, waiting for darkness and an opportunity to
free Rowdy. When they paused to breathe their horses,
loosening the saddle girths and giving the mounts respite

from the grueling trail, Rowdy put a question to his companion, and the Kid nodded his head.

"Yep, I heard enough," the Kid said. "I know now that it was Kelhorn and his boys who tackled the stagecoach and got the saddle. Those unbranded cayuses they were riding had kept me from being sure before, and, of course, I couldn't savvy then why Kelhorn should be wanting a kak so bad that he'd go in for masked robbery to get one. I still don't know what makes that saddle so valuable. Maybe you can tell me?"

"It's a long story," Rowdy said. "I'll spin it for you when we've got the time to spare. Right now we'd better start burning leather again. You figure on telling the sheriff that Kelhorn and his boys were the ones who were running around with flour sacks pulled over their heads?"

The Rimrock Kid shrugged. "Don't know as it would do much good," he observed as he tightened his saddle girth and set his foot in a stirrup. "Where's the proof?"

And that was the size of it. Kelhorn had accused the Kid of rustling Winged-H cattle, and Kelhorn had rigged a gun-trap for the wild horse hunter, yet Kelhorn had been unable to set the law against the Kid. Now the Rimrock Kid had satisfied himself that Kelhorn had tried his hand at masked robbery, but again it would be a case of one man's word against another. And doubtless the whole Winged-H crew would be equipped with a flock of alibis that would make the Kid look as though he'd had a touch of the sun. It was going to take more than hearsay evidence to tangle the twine of Jake Kelhorn. Yet tangle it they must. Perhaps, Rowdy reflected, tonight Kelhorn would go too far.

Hoisting himself into his saddle, Rowdy abruptly changed the subject. "That big brass bell at Hackett's place," he said. "It was rung just before food was fetched to me. Does the Winged-H always announce feeding time that way?"

The Kid gave Rowdy a queer, sidelong look, eloquent of the Kid's bewilderment as to why a man would be interested in brass bells at a time like this. "It's a supper bell," the Kid admitted. "When Hackett was a mite younger and more active, he was a bearcat for having his boys in the cook-shack on time. I've heard it told that that bell was rung promptly at six o'clock, and if a man didn't have his feet under the table pronto, he got potato peelings to eat. Why?"

But Rowdy was lifting his horse to a gallop again and the sudden clatter precluded any reply. Rowdy had learned something that he wanted to know, and through his mind was running a refrain:

"If the Devil's Saddle's too hot for your pants
    When the April sun is hell,
Injun down from that kak and bend your old back,
    When you hear your own supper bell . . ."

Before they reached Dryfooting, Rowdy was to find that that jingle, whirling around in a man's head, could make him dizzy, and he deliberately banished the verse. The Rimrock Kid once more taking the lead, they came to town before the evening was too old, and they found a clutter of buckboards and wagons before the ugly, square front of the opera house. Hitchrails of nearby establishments were lined to fullness.

It wasn't every night that Dryfooting had a show of the kind that Nathaniel Faust and Nan Bolton were scheduled to present, and the populace of the town and the neighboring badlands had turned out full force. Through the planking of the frame building, the raucous clangor of a brass band, a local aggregation, percolated; this band had

doubtless ballyhooed the show from the street before the
theater at an earlier hour. Obviously the performance had
already started; and the Kid would have pulled his horse
to a halt before the opera house if Rowdy hadn't laid a
hand upon his arm.

"The jail first," Rowdy said. "My partner's there, and
he's to be held until you tell Catastrophe Kate that we
told you last evening that we had the saddle and aimed to
return it to its owners. That's why I left that note at your
camp, asking you to report to the sheriff as soon as possible. We may need all the help we can get before this
night's over. Stumpy makes a good hand when there's
trouble in the wind."

The Kid nodded, and the two walked their lathered
mounts to the jail-building, dismounted, and jangled their
spurs inside. The sheriff's office to the front was dark and
deserted, but a lamp burned overhead in the cell corridor,
and there was light in Stumpy's cell. Light enough.
Rowdy, pausing before the barred door and peering
within, gasped in astonishment.

"Well," said Stumpy sourly, arising from the cell's cot.
"It's about time you got back. What did you do? Stop to
pick daisies?"

But Rowdy was still staring speechlessly, and it wasn't
Stumpy who was making Rowdy doubt his eyes. Stumpy
had remained unchanged; he was the same little man,
leathery and grizzled, with the same down-tilted mustache; but the cell had undergone a complete transforma-
tion in the hours since Rowdy had been in it. Flowery
curtains adorned its single barred window, the stool had a
lace-edged pillow upon it, and the cot, previously draped
by a tangle of moth-eaten blankets, older than the Rocky
Mountains, now had a spread so snowy white that it made
Rowdy blink. Besides this, the cell now contained a stand
upon which perched the largest cage Rowdy had ever

seen, and in this cage, glaring at him unblinkingly, was an owl. No mistaking it. An owl!

"What's that thing for?" Rowdy demanded, pointing a wavering finger.

"She couldn't get a canary," Stumpy explained.

"Does it *sing?*"

"Of course not. It's stuffed. Don't stand there with yore jaw dustin' the floor. What in thunderation kept you?"

Rowdy dragged his eyes from the stuffed owl, the flowered curtains, the festooned stool, and the transformed cot with an effort, restoring himself to the reality of the night and the need for action by a vigorous shaking of his head. "What happened can keep till later," he said. "Here's the Kid, and he can get you out of here. Where's the sheriff?"

"She's baking a cake for me," Stumpy said. "Shortly she's coming over to play cards."

"Then we'll have to find her and get this cell unlocked!"

"No need," Stumpy said placidly. "The door will open if you put yore hand to it."

"You mean the cell's unlocked?" Rowdy ejaculated and felt his senses reel.

"Shore," said Stumpy. "The sheriff says it's degrading to a man's soul to keep him under lock and key. She says that that puts him on a par with some caged jungle beast with none of the finer sensibilities which centuries of civilization have imparted to the race. Leastwise it was some such spiel as that."

Rowdy touched the cell door and, sure enough, it gave to his touch. He stared at this miracle of achievement, scarcely believing it, and, at his elbow, the Rimrock Kid chuckled, a sound real enough to be reassuring. "Come out of there, Stumpy," Rowdy said sternly. "Or have you been gazing at that owl so long that you're hypnotized?"

"I can't come," Stumpy said. "Katharine wouldn't like it."

"Katherine—?"

"Catastrophe Kate, some calloused characters call her. She's a fine woman, Rowdy, with a heart as big as a Percheron hoss. She left me here on my honor not to abuse the privileges she was showing me. She says I remind her of her third husband, Ebenezer. She met him at the funeral of her second husband, Sebastian. Or maybe it was the other way around. No, sir, I can't go busting my word to that good woman who's been providing me with the fust thing I ever had that approximated a home."

"Okay," said Rowdy and turned on his heel. "Jake Kelhorn and his crew are in town. They aim to bust up the show at the opera house tonight and get their hands on that saddle again. I was counting on your help, Stumpy. But if you won't have this pokey peeled off you any way but the right way, I just won't be able to spare the time. Keep your ears tuned, old hoss. You may hear some shooting a little later on."

"Now wait a minute!" Stumpy bawled and came charging into the corridor. "You ain't countin' me out on this deal, Rowdy. Danged if I ever knew a man so anxious to always hog the fun!"

Rowdy smiled grimly, opened the door to the sheriff's office at the head of the corridor, and felt his way into that darkened room. He was prowling through Catastrophe Kate's desk when Stumpy and the Rimrock Kid overtook him, and they waited in silence for a long moment until Stumpy said, "What you looking for?"

"Your gun," Rowdy said. "Likely the sheriff put it here when you were locked up. She fished mine out of this desk before I left town this afternoon."

Stumpy slapped his thigh. "Here's my gun," he said.

"In my holster. I had it in my cell with me, and I just went back now to get it. Katharine said I'd better keep it with me. She reckoned that when a feller was as used as I was to having a hog-leg around he'd be plumb uncomfortable without one. She's mighty considerate, that woman."

"Mighty," Rowdy agreed, no longer surprised at anything, and he felt for the street door.

They came down the steps together, the three of them, and without a word to each other, they fell into step, shoulder to shoulder, and chose the middle of the street for their march toward the opera house. They had no plan; they would handle the situation as it shaped itself. From the theater ahead came a thunder of applause and hoots and whistles, but even above this strident outburst the clangor of the brass band reached them, and Rowdy recognized the tune that was being played. *There'll Be a Hot Time in the Old Town Tonight.*

And that, Rowdy decided grimly, could be as prophetic as anything.

10

THE DEVIL'S SADDLE

To reach the opera house, the three had to pace almost the entire length of Dryfooting's main street, and Rowdy strode along feeling no more comfortable than a live fish in a frying pan. Jake Kelhorn, that bird of sinister plumage, might have posted a man in the street to guard against any interference in whatever scheme Kelhorn had in mind. But no man challenged the trio. Kelhorn, then, was presuming that Rowdy Dow was safely tied in the Winged-H blacksmith shop and that Stumpy Grampis was the county's unwilling guest in the local calaboose. And

the Rimrock Kid had not entered into Kelhorn's calculations tonight—at least not as a menace of any sizable caliber. The street was as safe as a fat lady's lap.

Still, Rowdy's eyes shuttled to left and right as they
advanced, scanning with particular care the shadowy slots
between buildings and lifting his glance to rooftops where
a man with a rifle might be posted. In this manner he
happened to give more than usual attention to one squat,
frame structure, and, making out the legend inscribed
upon its darkened, unwashed front window, he saw that it
was the home of *The Dryfooting Extra*, the cowtown's
newspaper.

He'd been aware of this institution the first time he'd
ever inventoried the street, but now he was reminded of
his talk with Caleb Hackett and of a reference to the
scorched journal of Captain Joshua Griffen, that ill-fated
Argonaut. According to Hackett, that journal had for years
been displayed in the window of yonder newspaper, and
Jake Kelhorn was supposed to be trying to find its present
whereabouts on behalf of his boss. That, Rowdy decided,
was something to think about.

From two points of view, Griffen's journal was likely
utterly worthless. A good deal of it had been destroyed by
fire when the Sioux had put the torch to the wagon train
after the massacre. Obviously any reference to the original hiding place of Griffen's legendary gold had been
burned. Otherwise earlier treasure-seekers would have
had an easy time finding the gold. And even if the document did contain a clue to where Griffen had buried his
treasure, that clue would now be of no value. Tennyson
Tolbert had found the gold and removed it. Yet a hunch
was growing in Rowdy, compelling as a wood tick in a
man's ear, and that hunch was that time spent scanning
Griffen's journal would not be wasted. He wondered if

The Dryfooting Extra still numbered the document among its possessions.

But this was not the moment to find out. There was other work to do, and Rowdy, making a mental note to see about the journal another time, dismissed the matter from his mind. The three reaching the opera house, they proceeded to the box-office and laid down the price of tickets. Here was irony for you, Rowdy reflected. Kill a couple of horses getting to town to protect a trouper from possible danger and you had to *pay* for the privilege of risking your hide! Justice was not only blind; she was grasping and avaricious. Tickets in hand, the three shouldered inside.

Rowdy grew wary again. Arriving thus belatedly, he anticipated coming into a packed auditorium where the audience, already seated, would have a good long look at the tardy trio as they threaded the aisle in search of seats. Kelhorn and his crew were likely inside—there'd been no time to examine the many hitchrails to search out Winged-H horses and be sure—and Kelhorn would see this entry of theirs. But luck favored the three. They entered the opera house between acts, and that made all the difference.

This theater was of the old-time frontier type, the kind that flourished in every mining camp pretentious enough to support one. Planking had replaced the sawdust floor of earlier days, but the seats that filled the vastness between the entrance door and the stage were loose wooden chairs which could be easily cleared away for dancing. Thus were the finances embellished in those arid periods when no traveling shows were on hand to grace the stage; and two other obvious sidelines likewise contributed to keeping the wolf from the opera house door. Along the sides of the big room ran the curve of curtained boxes where painted girls, their singing and dancing acts finished, beguiled the theater patrons into buying drinks for them. Rowdy, a traveled man, was familiar with that ancient business known as "rustling the boxes." Likewise he was familiar with the function of the bar which was maintained to the rear of the room, near the door through which the three had just entered.

It was the bar, or rather the wild rush to the bar, that cloaked their arrival. An act having ended, a high percentage of the patrons were now fighting their way up the aisles to slake a thirst that had apparently grown to tremendous proportions during the recent entertainment. With men tightly packed and jostling each other, Rowdy fought against this current of humanity, elbowing passage for Stumpy and the Kid. They found their way into an aisle and followed it half the length of the building before they eased into empty seats, Rowdy letting the other two precede him and taking the chair flanking the aisle. Patrons came drifting back to deserted seats, but no one laid claim to the three they'd preempted; and the show was ready to go on.

Rowdy cast a quick look around him. Here were more people than he'd supposed were ever crowded into Dryfooting at one time, much less into a single building. There were cowmen and their crews from outlying ranches, and a turnout of townspeople that made a cross-section of Dryfooting. Here was the local blacksmith, conspicuous in Sunday clothing into which he had obviously been poured and forgotten to say "when"; yonder sat the livery stable hostler, ultra-fragrant in this close confinement; beyond him was the town's medico. There was even a sprinkling of women. But if Kelhorn and his crew were here, they were not within the immediate range of Rowdy's vision.

The curtains were parting jerkily. Offstage, someone

manipulated the thunder box, thereby giving a not-too-convincing illusion of storm and hail. The orchestra struck up a fanfare in the pit and let it die of sheer ennui. The smoking footlights flared fitfully, fanned by the breeze of the curtains' parting. Rowdy judged that they had likely missed that laughable farce, *The Maid's Night Off*, which had opened the entertainment, and probably the banjo selections, scheduled to follow the skit, now belonged to the ages, too. As Rowdy recalled the program, Nan Bolton's act was third, and he hoped they hadn't missed it. He'd sampled the girl's skill once and had a hole in his hat to remember her by; he wanted now to see a more orthodox performance.

Nor was he disappointed. The opera house manager, a ponderous man whose clothes were outdated by a generation and a half, moved onto the stage, a wilted carnation drooping from his buttonhole. He lifted fat hands, beseeching silence, began to speak, remembered the cigar clamped between his rubbery lips and removed it.

"La-a-d-e-e-s, and gentle-m-e-e-n," he said. "At considerable expense we have brought here for you tonight an aggregation of talent of the kind likely to be found only in the larger metropolises of this and the Eur-o-peen continent. And now it is with great pride that I present an act that has enthralled and held spellbound the crowned heads of many countries. La-a-d-e-e-s and gentle-m-e-e-n, I give you the greatest sharpshooter of all time, that beautiful young lady, fresh from a lengthy engagement in Noo-o-o Yawk City—Miss Nan Bolton!"

The band put more vigor into a second fanfare, the manager, his cigar restored, lumbered off the stage, and from the wings Nan came skipping to make a quick bow. Feet stomped lustily, a thunder of applause lifted to the ceiling, and men whistled wildly. Out of this hurly-burly of sound came someone's cry: "Whatcha doing after the show tonight?" Nan's smile stayed professional; she had a way of remaining personable yet wrapping dignity around her like a protecting cloak. She was, Rowdy decided, quite a girl.

He cast a glance at the Rimrock Kid and saw that the face of the wild horse hunter had softened. But Stumpy was not so entranced as to have forgotten their real purpose here. That leathery little man was alternately shifting his glance from the stage to such of the audience as he could see. Rowdy grinned contentedly. The blandishments of a jail transformed had done no irreparable damage to the soul of Stumpy Grampis. A man could still count on Stumpy when the need came.

Rowdy's attention was again drawn to the stage. Nathaniel Faust had appeared from the wings, toting, with the help of the manager, a gun case containing several rifles of different calibers, and at least two shotguns. Following this came a table loaded with various sorts of paraphernalia. From this table Faust selected a cigar, lighted it, drew lustily upon it until he had a half inch of ash, and then took a stand at one end of the stage. Nan moved soundlessly to the rack, selected a rifle of light caliber, moved the width of the stage away from the man, and quickly lifted the rifle and fired. Her first shot was a miss; she paused, looking around her as if to gauge the difference in light from that which she was used to, squeezed trigger again, and the cigar took on a splintered shapelessness.

Rowdy was suddenly all interest. He'd traveled too widely, had Rowdy, to be as naive as he sometimes chose to appear, and he recognized here a real talent made sharper through constant, unending practice. The rare skill of the immortal Annie Oakley had brought a rash of feminine sharpshooters to the American stage, and even when Annie Oakley had made her first professional appearance there were at least sixteen women doing havoc to various targets on the paying side of smoking footlights. Rowdy had witnessed more than one display of this kind —and thereby gotten a vast skepticism for professional marksmen in general and lady sharpshooters in particular.

No other type of performance offered as many possibilities for colossal fakery as stage marksmanship. Take the act of shooting the ash from a cigar, for instance. Rowdy had once lost a bet in a Colorado mining town as to whether a certain Dead Eye Dan, appearing at the camp's theater, could do that particular trick. Rowdy's money had said that Dead Eye Dan was an imposter of the first water. And Rowdy's money had gone into another's pocket. Whereupon Rowdy had waylaid Dead Eye Dan in the alley behind the theater after the performance, and persistent dunkings in a community horse trough had elicited the information from Dead Eye Dan that his assistant had had only to jiggle between his teeth a hairpin which had been shoved through the body of the cigar. That slight movement had spilled the ashes simultaneously with the firing of a blank shot from Dead Eye's never-failing rifle. Rowdy, a poorer man that night, was at least a wiser one.

But Nan's bullet had done more than drop the ashes from the cigar in Faust's mouth. It had splintered the cigar, and therefore Rowdy was convinced that he'd seen real shooting. And thus it was with avid interest that he followed the rest of the act, seeing her knock a small cork from the bottom of a glass held in Faust's steady hand, seeing her change from one type of gun to another and show mastery of all of them. Composition balls were burst in the air over the audience's head, and the manager, with a poor show of bravado, allowed an apple to be ruined atop his bald cranium with Miss Bolton outdoing William Tell at his own game.

Once this girl had told Rowdy that she hadn't been shooting for keeps when Kelhorn and his men, hooded and desperate, had attacked the troupers' stagecoach out in the badlands. Rowdy believed it now.

The act ended all too soon, ended in a storm of applause that was tinged with respect. Laughable farces and banjo overtures might not be meat and drink to Dryfooting's populace, but here was something they could understand—a superlative skill with guns. Their insistent applause earned them an encore and another, but after that the manager lumbered out upon the stage again, held up his fat hands for the long moment it took to earn silence, remembered his cigar and removed it, and beamed benignly. The manager, it was obvious, had justified his existence upon the planet this night.

"La-a-d-e-e-s, and gentle-m-e-e-n," he said. "At considerable expense we have brought here for you tonight an aggregation of talent of the kind likely to be found only in the larger metropolises of this and the Eur-o-peen continent . . ."

Stumpy, seated next to Rowdy, gazed at the stage in rapt fascination. "The man's a danged parrot!" Stumpy whispered. "He said them same words before!"

"And now," said the manager, "it is with great pride that I present an act that has enthralled and held spellbound the crowned heads of many countries. La-a-d-e-e-s and gentle-m-e-e-n, I give you the world renowned Professor Marvelo, that master of magic and legerdemain who is fresh from a lengthy engagement in Noo-o-o Yawk City. And, as a special treat for the citizens of Dryfooting, Professor Marvelo has condescended to perform an act seldom attempted on this or any other stage—his prize act, *The Devil's Saddle*. You have seen magicians adept at making small articles disappear. You shall now witness a feat surpassing anything of the sort. Before your ver-ry eyes a saddle shall vanish into thin air. La-a-d-e-es and gentle-m-e-e-n—Professor Marvelo!"

The orchestra raised a rumpus, the manager betook himself from the stage, and Professor Marvelo glided from the wings. There was no doubt but what Professor Marvelo and Nathaniel Faust were one and the same, though now a long gown clothed the man, making him appear even taller. This gown was black, and, emblazoned upon it in silver were stars and moons and signs of the zodiac. Surmounting Faust's silvery hair was a tall, pointed cap, likewise emblazoned. Raising those slender, eloquent hands of his, Faust said, "I shall require two assistants from the audience. Who will volunteer, please?"

Feet shuffled self-consciously throughout the theater, a pair of chairs scraped at the back of the room, and two men stepped down the aisle. Stumpy Grampis sucked in a long breath. "The flour sack boys!" he hissed.

For it was two of Jake Kelhorn's crew who were approaching the stage, and Stumpy had recognized them from that episode in the Tarantula when the crew had rigged a gun-trap for the Rimrock Kid. The Winged-H hands were not wearing flour sack hoods at the moment, of course; they strode purposefully down the aisle, found steps to the stage and mounted these. And Rowdy, who'd marked from whence they had come, craned his neck and saw now that Kelhorn and the three others who drew Winged-H pay were still seated to the back of the room.

Professor Marvelo was raising those slender hands again. "Since our program is running behind time, due to Miss Bolton's so graciously conceding to encores, I am dispensing with the first part of my act and proceeding at once to the feat which is our major attraction. The disappearing Devil's Saddle."

He snapped his fingers, and a flower magically blossomed within his hand. He fastened the flower in the shirt-front of one of the Winged-H hardcases who flanked him on either side, and, at the same time, since the snapping of his fingers had obviously been a cue, the manager appeared from the wings, shoving before him a small, black tent, apparently made of velvet, a four-cornered affair which, Rowdy judged, was held erect by wire riggings. This tent, high enough to conceal a man, was moved to a position in the exact center of the stage.

"And now," said Faust, "will one of you gentlemen be so kind as to step inside this tent and examine it?"

He held open the flap so that the audience could glimpse the dark, narrow interior; and one of the Winged-H volunteers gingerly ventured inside, turned around a time or two and emerged. Faust snapped his fingers again, a second flower appeared and was fastened upon the second volunteer, and the manager came from the wings toting a saddle that was all too familiar to Rowdy Dow.

"The Devil's Saddle," Faust said in a voice of sepulchral awe that still managed to carry to the entire audience. "An article of a kind familiar to all of you. And now—" He gestured to the second volunteer. "—will you be so kind as to examine this saddle and assure the audience that it is indeed what it seems to be, an ordinary saddle as far as the eye can tell."

The Winged-H man approached the saddle with a marked avidness, and within Rowdy there was an impulse to cry out a warning, to shout to Faust to be on his guard. Faust had seen these two men before, out in the badlands, but they'd been masked then, and Faust had no way of now recognizing them. But the man kneeling beside the saddle was only doing as he'd been directed, feeling the

saddle, thumping it, hoisting it for weight. This hardcase
nodded to the audience, a gesture to indicate his satisfaction that the saddle was what it was represented to be.

"Place it inside the tent," Faust ordered.

The saddle was lifted, set upon the floor of the stage
inside the tent, and the Winged-H men stepped back and
stood watching.

"The tent shall now be laced shut," Faust announced.
"Not by myself, but by these men who are known to all of
you. Thereafter I shall say the magic words of the ancient
Chaldeans, and with those words the saddle shall dissolve
into thin air. Gentlemen—" He glanced at his two assistants. "—will you be so kind as to lace the flap of the
tent."

Stumpy was tugging frantically at Rowdy's elbow.
"Kelhorn!" Stumpy hissed. *"He's left!"*

Rowdy swiveled his head; for a moment his attention
had been glued to the stage and held there by the persua-
sive voice of Nathaniel Faust. Now he saw that another in
that row of chairs that had been occupied by the
Winged-H crew was empty. Kelhorn was indeed leaving,
the man was just disappearing through the doorway
leading into the lobby. Instantly Rowdy was upon his
feet.

"Cover my back," he whispered to Stumpy. "Whatever's going to happen is going to happen now. I'm counting on you to keep the rest of those galoots off me. I'll
take care of Kelhorn!"

11

Anything could happen now—and likely would. Such was Rowdy's thought as he went hurrying up the aisle, hard on the heels of the vanishing Jake Kelhorn. Good luck and wild riding had gotten Rowdy to Dryfooting before Kelhorn had chosen the moment in which to make his play; after that Rowdy's strategy had been to bide his own time, waiting for Kelhorn's move. The disadvantage was that Rowdy hadn't the slightest idea what Winged-H's foreman was up to. Kelhorn wanted the saddle, and Kelhorn meant to get it, but now, oddly, the man had turned his back upon the object of his desperate desire. As Rowdy saw it, the chore was to keep Kelhorn in sight, and let the chips fall where they might.

The chief obstacle to Rowdy's simple plan was likely to be the other Winged-H hands, that hardcase lot who were ranged along a row of seats to the rear of the auditorium. With two on the stage and Kelhorn gone, there were only three who were in a position to bar Rowdy's way—but they could be three too many. Stumpy and the Rimrock Kid were on the alert, ready to lend a hand if Rowdy needed it, but Rowdy hoped there'd be no need for assistance. Any kind of delay might be disastrous. Jake Kelhorn, who was moving along as though he had firecrackers in the seat of his pants, had to be overtaken.

Lady Luck, that fickle female, smiled upon Rowdy now. He went up the aisle unchallenged; the three Winged-H men had their eyes avidly glued to the stage where their two confederates, as Rowdy saw by a hasty glance over his shoulder, were busily engaged in lacing shut the flap of the queer black tent under the direction of Professor

Marvelo. A hushed expectancy held the audience; all attention was focused on the stage, and Rowdy grinned with the thought that he might have gone somersaulting along the aisle without attracting any attention to himself.

His grin faded as he got out into the lobby, for the only person who met his eye was the ticket-taker, a plump youth with slickered-down hair who was most obviously the manager's offspring. Jake Kelhorn was gone. Out into the street? If that were the case, looking for him would be akin to the highly touted search for the elusive needle in the broad haystack. Rowdy took a spread-legged stand before the ticket-taker and said grimly, "A man just passed this way. Which direction did he head?"

"I—I didn't see anybody," the youth quavered.

That was where the lad made his mistake. Anything else in the way of an elusive answer might have sent Rowdy on into the street, unsuspecting, but this youngster's flat denial of having seen anybody was obviously a lie. Jake Kelhorn was most definitely big enough to be visible to the naked eye. Rowdy donned a look that would have scared a rattlesnake out of a year's growth. Scowling, he wrapped a hand in the youth's shirt-front and twisted until buttons popped. Lifting the fellow from his feet, he shook the ticket-taker vigorously.

"Lying," said Rowdy, "is a bad habit. It will keep you from getting into heaven, and it will get you into a heap of trouble here on earth. Jake Kelhorn must have bribed you to keep your mouth buttoned. How much did he give you?"

"F-f-five dollars," the youth managed to say.

"I'll give you ten to line up on my side."

Whether it was the possibility of now playing both ends against a middle and reaping fifteen dollars for his trouble, or whether it was the fear of further violence at Rowdy's hands, there was no telling, but suddenly this plump youth was most willing to talk. "It was Kelhorn all right," he said. "He gave me five dollars to tell him how to get under the stage."

"Under the stage?"

"He said that he wanted to play a little joke. He promised there'd be no harm done and that I wouldn't get into trouble on account of it."

Rowdy released his grip on the ticket-taker and ran his finger inside the top of his right boot and by this means fished out a sheaf of bills that were folded neatly and pressed flat. The Winged-H crew had missed this windfall in any search they'd made of him while he was unconscious that afternoon. Peeling off a ten, Rowdy held it up to view.

"And how do you get under the stage?" he demanded.

The youth hesitated, his Adam's apple bobbing as his eyes lifted to Rowdy's grim face and lowered to the ten dollar bill. "There's two ways," he said. "A door gives in from the orchestra pit, and another door leads to the basement from here in the lobby. That door yonder."

He was pointing to a shadowy corner, and Rowdy was already heading in that direction. Kelhorn, then, hadn't suspected that he was being followed; Kelhorn's bribe to the boy in the lobby had been to gain information, and that youth, belabored by a guilty conscience, had instinctively lied when approached regarding the whereabouts of Kelhorn. Rowdy got the indicated door open and found himself at the head of a shadowy stairs. He descended gingerly and came into the nether world of the theater. This basement was one vast room, the near end of it filled with dusty flies and rolled backdrops and other paraphernalia designed for mysterious purposes beyond Rowdy's understanding. But, far ahead, in the region that would be directly beneath the stage, a lantern burned dimly upon a box. And the light it cast revealed a weird and silent struggle that brought Rowdy running hastily forward, heedless of the unsound footing in this dusty dungeon.

Nan Bolton was down here. She must have come by way of the entrance from the orchestra pit, Rowdy judged. Nan was here, and so was the Devil's Saddle, lying spilled upon the floor. How the saddle had gotten here was most obvious, and explained the means by which Professor Marvelo worked this particular feat of magic. There was a trapdoor in the center of the stage, a trapdoor which could be released from beneath the stage, and a short step-ladder provided access to whatever fastening held the trapdoor. Thus, when the saddle was placed inside the tent and the flap fastened so that the saddle was no longer visible, Nan, in the role of assistant to her grandfather, having previously stationed herself here while the oldster was holding the rapt attention of the audience, had had merely to lower the saddle through the trapdoor, thus creating the illusion of the saddle's having vanished when the tent flap was later opened and the interior of the tent exposed.

And this Nan had done. She'd gotten the saddle and lowered it to the floor, but whatever she was supposed to do next was not being done—and for a very good reason. Jake Kelhorn was here, and Kelhorn's intent was to lay his hands upon the saddle, but the girl was giving him a fight. Smothered in his arms, she was clawing frantically at his face and pitting all of her wiry strength against him. And thus they struggled silently; Kelhorn had managed to clamp a heavy hand across Nan's mouth, while the man himself was striving to make a minimum of noise so as not to bring help from above.

The ceiling of the basement rustled to the nervous feet of the audience; now the brass band almost directly overhead began a great clanging, probably on cue from the stage. With this fanfare blaring, Rowdy came charging forward. He got Kelhorn by one shoulder and swung him around and planted a fist in the man's swarthy face. This was Kelhorn's first inkling that an intruder was present, and a mighty hard way of finding out it proved to be. And Kelhorn's great astonishment when he recognized his assailant indicated that he hadn't glimpsed Rowdy in the audience. Patently, Jake Kelhorn had supposed that Rowdy was still lying in the Winged-H blacksmith shop.

But Kelhorn was not the kind who swooned from surprise. His hand dropped instantly toward his holster, and his gun cleared leather, but Rowdy was upon the foreman, his fingers clamping around Kelhorn's wrist. Rowdy twisted hard, and the gun fell to the floor. Kicking the weapon aside, Rowdy took a quick, backward step and measured Kelhorn's chin. Rowdy's fist came up from the vicinity of his knees, but that gave Kelhorn time to see the blow coming, and he dodged aside, Rowdy's knuckles grazing his shoulder and spinning him about.

Rowdy's own gun swung in the holster at his hip—the gun the Winged-H crew had taken from him today but which had been returned to him by the Rimrock Kid. Rowdy might have gotten that gun out of leather and put an end to all this with a minimum of effort, but red wrath was dancing in Rowdy's brain. He was remembering himself trussed and helpless on the floor of the Winged-H bunkhouse, and Jake Kelhorn planting a kick against his ribs. He was remembering his natural antipathy for this man, an antipathy that had first been born in the Tarantula when Kelhorn had rigged a gun-trap for the Rimrock Kid. Here, Rowdy decided angrily, was a chance to teach Jake Kelhorn some manners. Besides, it had cost ten dollars to buy into this fight, and a man had to get his money's worth.

Nan had stooped and gotten hold of the gun Rowdy had twisted from Kelhorn's hand; she came erect with that gun leveled. She had the drop on Kelhorn, and this could have been the end of the struggle, but Rowdy grunted: "My meat, Miss!" And he launched a barrage of blows at Kelhorn, his fists beating against the man's broad face and beefy body like hail on a tin roof. Nan still kept the gun, but she flattened herself against a wall and held the gun laxly. Now there, Rowdy decided, was a girl who knew how to get along with a man!

But this was no time for reflection upon the multiple merits of Miss Nan Bolton. Jake Kelhorn was giving Rowdy a handful. Kelhorn was heavily muscled and could make a blow count, and Kelhorn understood, too, that this was to be a finish fight between them, with no outside interference. That Kelhorn might find himself looking down the business end of a gun-barrel in Nan's hand even if he did succeed in overcoming Rowdy was obvious, but Kelhorn was apparently satisfied that he could cope with the girl once he'd polished off Rowdy. Assurance was in his dark eyes. He came at Rowdy like a runaway train, but Rowdy merely stepped off the track, hooking a left at Kelhorn's jaw as the man swept past him. The blow almost derailed Kelhorn.

But Kelhorn recovered himself quickly, so quickly that he smashed his knuckles against Rowdy's ear, a blow that made Rowdy feel as though he had a head full of hornets. Kelhorn closed with him then; the two went down in a wild tussle, rolling over and over on the dusty floor. Rowdy felt his shirt shred beneath Kelhorn's pawing hands; Winged-H's foreman got a thumb into Rowdy's eye and started gouging. But Rowdy broke the man's grip, rolled Kelhorn under him, and managed to get to his own feet.

Rough and tumble was not the way to best Jake Kelhorn. The man had a superiority of weight and muscle. This Rowdy knew, just as he knew that he must pin his own faith in fancy footwork, making it an illusive battle of hitting and running. He let Jake Kelhorn get to a stand. The man thrust up an awkward guard, and Rowdy feinted his way through it. Kelhorn launched a wild, pile-driver punch that would have floored a steer, but Rowdy ducked under it. And, ducking, he saw Kelhorn's jaw temptingly exposed and put all his strength into an assault upon that rugged fortress. His left fist smashed at the jaw, his right fist made a repeat performance as Kelhorn went down. And Kelhorn did go down, sprawling his length upon the dusty floor and lying immobile. Thus, suddenly, was the fight finished.

Nan's eyes were shining in the semi-darkness. "For a man your size, you tie a neat package," she said.

Rowdy's chest was behaving like a blacksmith's bellows, and perspiration glued the remnants of his shirt to him. He touched Kelhorn with his toe. "Know this gent?"

"I've seen him once before," she said. "The day before yesterday we played a little town called Willow, up north on the Missouri. This fellow and four or five friends were in the front row when we put on our performance."

"That," said Rowdy, "explains a couple of things. Now I know how he guessed how the disappearing saddle act was worked and was able to lay his plans tonight. And it also explains why he was hot on your trail when you came through the badlands from Willow yesterday. This jigger is the head of the flour sack boys, and he's the one who packed off your saddle. Jake Kelhorn, here, is a man with a one-track mind."

Nan said, "You've proved you're a friend. The apology I made in the jail this morning hasn't got any strings on it now."

Overhead, the brass band suddenly ceased its clanging. Rowdy raised his eyes aloft. "What's next?"

"The show goes on," Nan said. "Grandfather uses me in

this part of his act. While the band was playing, he was going through a long rigamarole and making passes with his hands at that tent. He always draws that part of it out until he gets the audience worked up. Now he's opening the tent and showing them that the saddle has gone."

Rowdy grinned. "And shortly he'll tie the flap again. And you'll push the saddle back up through the trapdoor. Is that it? The whole thing's so simple that I'm wondering why I didn't catch on pronto as to how it was done."

"The simpler an act, the more likely it is to fool an audience," Nan said. "But you're wrong about my passing the saddle back through the trapdoor. Grandfather is standing at the footlights right now. He's saying, 'Where the devil is the Devil's Saddle?' When he's repeated that about five times, I'll come down the aisle from the front of the theater carrying the saddle. That's the climax to the act. The wise-acres in the audience will have already figured out that the saddle is supposed to appear back in the tent. They get a surprise when it shows up at the opposite end of the theater."

Rowdy's grin widened. "Come on," he said. "We'll give 'em twice as much for their money as they've hoped to get. I'll show them a little magic of my own."

He picked the kak from the floor and handed it to her. Then he stooped, grasped one of Kelhorn's limp arms, and, by a mighty effort, got the unconscious man over one of his shoulders. It took another effort to get to his feet with such a load—Kelhorn was obviously not stuffed with popcorn—but Rowdy was able to stagger along behind the girl. She quickly led the way through the shadowy basement; they came up the stairs to the lobby, and when they made their appearance above, the girl with the saddle, Rowdy with his own burden, the ticket-taker took on the stricken look of one who witnesses a particularly disreputable ghost. Rowdy gave the youth a comforting wink.

Nan had stepped into the auditorium; Rowdy was at her heels. Yonder, on the stage, stood the two Winged-H hands, and yonder, too, was Professor Marvelo, intoning: "Where the devil is the Devil's Saddle?" His seamed face wore a look of concern which indicated that Nan had failed to be on hand at the proper cue. In fact, Rowdy judged that the perplexed Professor Marvelo had been about to ask, "Where in *hell* is the Devil's Saddle?" But Faust was saying nothing now, only staring. And his fixed gaze caused every head in the audience to swivel.

Down the aisle came Nan, bearing the illusive saddle, and behind her came Rowdy Dow, toting the unconscious form of Jake Kelhorn. And the sight was a signal that turned bedlam loose.

The two Winged-H hands on the stage recognized Rowdy and their boss, and the hardcase pair instinctively reached for guns. Rowdy was suddenly aware that he was to be a target, and equally aware that he was too encumbered to do a good job of defending himself. But there was no need for that. Stumpy Grampis was on his feet, a gun in his horny hand. And Stumpy's first shot hoisted a sombrero from the head of one of the men on the stage and sent the Stetson winging. The Rimrock Kid had come to a stand, also, his voice lifting stridently. "The first man to crack a cap stops a slug!" he shouted.

Everybody was on his feet now; the theater had turned into an uproarious pandemonium of shouting, gesticulating men, each demanding to know the wherefore behind this act that had been unscheduled and was providing extra dramatics. Some pressed into the aisles, clogging them, and Rowdy, craning his neck, saw the three Winged-H men who'd been sitting to the back of the theater making a wild bolt for the lobby. The two on the stage, thoroughly intimidated by Stumpy's gun, were darting for the wings. And, from out of nowhere, Catastrophe Kate had appeared and was hewing a path along the main aisle toward Rowdy. Perhaps it was the unexpected presence of the law that really turned the tide, but the Winged-H had most definitely decided upon retreat, leaving Jake Kelhorn to his fate.

"What kind of monkey business is this?" Catastrophe Kate was demanding as she thrust forward.

Rowdy dumped the unconscious Kelhorn at her broad feet. "Here's a customer for your calaboose," he said with a grin. "This time we've got him dead to rights. Miss Bolton will tell you that he just made a try at stealing the saddle again. Don't look so disappointed, ma'am. It's not me you're going to lock up this time. Better get those keys to jangling."

Up front, the manager was hastily ringing down the curtain. The patrons of the opera house had had all the theatricals they were going to get tonight.

12

A MAN AND HIS WORK

They were gathered in the sheriff's office to the front of the jail-building—Rowdy Dow and Stumpy Grampis and Catastrophe Kate, herself, the latter looking a little bewildered, for one of the firmer foundations of her belief had been sorely shaken tonight. She'd actually found an ex-outlaw who was not above doing the law's work. She'd even apologized to Rowdy, but not until Jake Kelhorn had been safely locked in one of the cells—*not* the cell with all the fancy fooforaw which had been provided for Stumpy. Rowdy, sitting in the sheriff's own chair with his legs crossed comfortably upon the sheriff's own desk, was in a fine good humor.

"Don't take on so, Sheriff," he said. "It isn't going to ruin your reputation just because you had a little outside help. I'd call it a good night's work all around."

Catastrophe Kate, seated in a straight-backed chair, brushed a wisp of rusty gray from her forehead and regarded Rowdy with a mixture of respect and die-hard suspicion. "Just the same, you could tell a heap more than you have," she said. "What gave you the notion, for instance, that there'd be trouble at the opera house tonight? And how did you know you'd find Kelhorn under the stage? Was *he* the head of those hooded galoots you told me about, the ones who stopped the stagecoach in the badlands and afterward tried to steal the saddle from the Seraglio?"

Rowdy grinned widely. "What hooded galoots?" he demanded. "There wasn't a lick of truth to that story about somebody putting a ladder up to our window. Remember? You said so yourself. It was impossible for anything like that to have happened without the whole hotel waking up."

Catastrophe Kate frowned. "You won't tell me the rest of it?"

"Look," said Rowdy. "I'm just a feller trying to do a job and turn an honest dollar. It will please me mightily to have Jake Kelhorn on ice for a while; it will give me more elbow room in these badlands. Nan Bolton will testify that he was trying to steal the saddle tonight and that he got mighty rough while doing it. That should keep him here at least thirty days."

Stumpy, perched upon the edge of the desk, said, "Let him do business his own way, Katharine. He'll show you his hand when the time comes."

Dryfooting's sheriff sighed in resignation, then fixed

her glance upon Stumpy. "I suppose that's all I can do," she said. "But I must say that I'm disappointed in you, Gabriel."

"*Gabriel*—!" Rowdy ejaculated. He'd ridden many miles with Stumpy Grampis and never dreamed that the little man possessed a Christian name.

"I left you here on your honor, Gabriel," Kate went on. "Yes, you've explained why you had to break your word to me and leave the cell. But you might have come to my cottage and got me to go to the opera house with you boys. As it was, I wouldn't even have been in on the finish if I hadn't found your cell empty, started looking for you and had a peek in the opera house just about the time the fireworks started."

Stumpy took on an extremely sorrowful look; even his down-tilted mustache drooped more dejectedly than of yore. "Rowdy fetched the Rimrock Kid to town. I sorta figgered that that cleared me, Katharine."

"Such things have to be done in proper form," Kate said sternly. "Tomorrow morning there'll be an official hearing of the case against you two. When it's over, you'll be legally free. You'll have the Rimrock Kid here to testify?"

"I'll see that he stays in town," Rowdy said. "Likely he's at the Seraglio right now, with Nan and her grandfather. They've got rooms there, and, after the ruckus, the Kid thought they needed safe escort to the hotel."

He swung his long legs to the floor and came to a stand. "We'll be getting along now. Me, I could use another shirt."

"Gabriel," Catastrophe Kate said, her eyes still on Stumpy, "you won't fail me again? You'll be at that hearing in the morning? Next to a drinking man, I simply can't abide an undependable man."

Stumpy swept off his sombrero with a flourish. "You

can count on me, Katharine. You can bet your bottom dollar."

"Come along," Rowdy said firmly.

Into the street, the partners found it comparatively quiet; the long queue of buckboards and wagons before the opera house had vanished as the badland ranchers, the performance abruptly terminated, had taken themselves and their families homeward. A good many saddle horses still lined hitchrails, but these were before the saloons which were ablaze and roaring. The two came to the Seraglio and found Bert Beecham, the rotund proprietor, presiding behind the desk.

"We left our war-sack in the room we had," Rowdy said. "We'd like to get it. Likewise we'd like to have the room again."

Beecham, who'd been forced to stay at his post and had thus missed the performance at the opera house, had since heard so many garbled accounts of what had happened that his head was spinning. He eyed the partners with a visible lack of enthusiasm and said, "I thought you two were in jail."

"They had to let us out," Rowdy explained. "Stumpy was giving the place a bad name."

Beecham reluctantly extended a key. "No shooting in the middle of the night," he pleaded.

"Wouldn't dream of it," Rowdy said. Leaning against the desk, he began shaping a cigarette. "See you've got a newspaper in town. *The Dryfooting Extra.* Odd name for a newspaper."

"Not for Art Billings's paper," Beecham said. "You see, Art runs his paper just opposite to most editors. Take the average sheet, it comes out regular, once a day or once a week as the case may be. If some big news breaks between regular publication times, the paper puts out an extra. But not Art. The only issues he puts out are extras. In between times there just ain't any newspaper."

"Now there's a notion for you," Rowdy observed. "Must give him a lot of spare time."

"That's the idea," Beecham said. "A great fellow for fishing, Art is. He'd rather wet a line than get a news story any day."

"A man worth knowing," Rowdy decided. "I'll look him up tomorrow."

"Won't do you a mite of good. Art's gone up to the Missouri for a week. There isn't a soul over at his place."

"Too bad," said Rowdy and headed for the stairs.

He'd learned exactly what he'd wanted to learn. He might have gotten this same information from Catastrophe Kate, and by the same subterfuge, but he hadn't wanted to betray any interest in the newspaper to the sheriff. That might prove embarrassing at a later day.

Into the room which was unchanged from yesterday, except for the bullet hole in the door, Rowdy delved into the war-sack and found a clean shirt. This he exchanged for the one Kelhorn had damaged, and, while he made the change, he took this opportunity, his first, to tell Stumpy all that had transpired today. He spoke of his search for the Rimrock Kid's camp. He mentioned the impulse that had then taken him to the Winged-H, told of Pablo Diablo and Caleb Hackett, a prisoner in his own ranch house, and of Tennyson Tolbert's letter with its riddle in rime. Also he told of his capture by Kelhorn's crew and his escape. Stumpy listened in attentive silence.

"Then you was right all the way along," Stumpy conceded. "Right as rain. And we *are* working for Hackett."

"And, like I told the sheriff, we've now got elbow room to work in," Rowdy said. "Kelhorn is after Griffen's gold, and Kelhorn is convinced that the saddle has the secret of its whereabouts. But Kelhorn will be cooling for a while.

Meantime, I'm going to have a look at Griffen's journal. Probably I'm loco, but I've got a hunch that it will tell me something I want to know."

"You figger the Winged-H boys will lay low tonight?"

Rowdy shrugged. "Hard telling. They didn't get the saddle, and they've lost Jake to the law. They can't very well quit now." He delved into the war-sack again, and this time he fished from it a ponderous, many-bladed jackknife. "Keep the home fires burning, Stumpy. Nan and her grandfather are in this hotel. Probably they've got the saddle here. The Rimrock Kid may still be with them, but I want you around if anything happens tonight. I won't be gone long."

Stumpy nodded obediently, and Rowdy left the room and strode along the hall. He passed one door and heard laughter beyond it, and it was the laughter of Nan Bolton. A babble of voices arose—the voices of Nathaniel Faust and the Kid. Rowdy smiled and went on to the stairs.

Reaching the street, he gave a careful look to left and right and then strolled the boardwalk until he came abreast of the office of *The Dryfooting Extra*. The building was as dark as it had been when it had drawn Rowdy's attention earlier tonight; he paused here, shaping up another cigarette, and looking for all the world like a man with nothing on his mind. But the flare of his match revealed that the front door of the establishment was held fast by a ponderous padlock. Rowdy moved on down the street and made himself disappear between two buildings.

He came thus to the alleyway and threaded its dark rancidness to the rear of the newspaper building. Here touch became the only sense that adequately served him, but nimble fingers soon told him that here was a window which refused to yield, and a door held fast by a padlock of the same gigantic proportions of the one to the front.

The jackknife came from his pocket, and he opened a needle-thin blade. With this he probed at the lock for all of ten minutes, and then gave up the effort. The blade was snapped shut and another opened so that Rowdy then had a serviceable screw driver in his hand.

It has been said that there are more ways than one to braid a horse's tail.

The door was hung upon two ponderous hinges, and, whereas the hasp that held the padlock to the door was riveted into place, the hinges were fastened by screws. Working quickly and silently, his ears constantly tuned for the sound of any drunken wayfarer who might come stumbling into the alley, Rowdy soon removed the screws and freed the hinges from their mooring. Now he was able to drag open the door a space, opening it on the opposite side from which it was intended to be opened, and he eased himself inside the building and hauled the door shut behind him.

The darkness lay so thick that Rowdy could almost feel it between fingers and thumb; an inky smell pervaded the atmosphere, and, as he moved carefully forward, he almost collided with a large hand press. He proceeded even more carefully after that; a type case was imperiled, but his ready hands kept it from falling. Much groping found for him a door giving into the front of the building, which was the office. It was not so dark here, for some light percolated through the unwashed bay window from the street.

For a full sixty seconds Rowdy merely stood, letting his eyes grow more accustomed to the darkness. Now he saw an ancient desk with tiers of bulging pigeon-holes perched atop it. There was a swivel chair and a safe, and it was the safe that interested Rowdy. It stood in the shadowiest corner, and he knelt before it and fingered the dial. Caleb Hackett had said that Griffen's journal had long been on display in the newspaper office's window. Since it was no longer there, it followed that it had been removed to safer keeping. Rowdy continued manipulating the dial, his ear pressed close to the safe's hard surface as he listened for the fall of the tumblers.

Here was one of those dubious skills which Rowdy had acquired in earlier years and was presumed to have put behind him when a governor's pardon had made him a free man. Yet Rowdy worked now at an old trade with no qualms of conscience. Knowledge, a sage had said, is wealth. A man, then, would be a plain fool to discard knowledge just because he'd taken to a straighter path. In fact, as Rowdy saw it, it would be a downright sin to throw away a skill so obviously useful!

And so Rowdy toiled for all of a half hour, pausing only to wipe his fingers upon his shirt whenever perspiration made them sticky. At times he almost despaired of success, wondering then if his old touch was gone. Then the door gave and he was able to swing it open. Grunting with satisfaction, Rowdy spent a moment listening. Boots were beating along the boardwalk, but the sound dwindled away and was lost. He had to risk a match now, and he did; the light flared and was cupped quickly in his hands, and Rowdy stared wildly at a legend he saw inscribed upon the safe's door:

NOTICE TO BURGLARS:

THIS SAFE CONTAINS PAPERS AND LEDGERS VALUABLE ONLY TO THE OWNER. IT IS USED TO PROTECT THESE ARTICLES FROM FIRE. DON'T BOTHER BLOWING THE THING OPEN TO SEE WHETHER I'M LYING. THE COMBINATION IS R4—L7—R6—R4. HELP YOURSELF!

Rowdy Dow kept his voice to a whisper, but he turned the air blue!

He began carefully to go through the contents of the safe. There was indeed nothing of value here, but he had to risk many matches as he examined objects which might have been Griffen's journal. None of them proved to be that historical curio. But one notebook, containing certain statistics on the weight of fish, the kind of fly used in catching said fish, had a slip of paper thrust between the pages as a sort of bookmark. Rowdy drew in his breath as he examined this paper. It was a receipt from the State Historical Society at Helena for one item described as "a journal purporting to be an account made by Captain Joshua Griffen . . ."

So that's what had become of the elusive journal!

Very carefully Rowdy restored the notebook and the receipt to the safe in the exact position he'd found it. Just as carefully he locked the safe, fumbled for the burnt match sticks he'd strewn about, pocketed these, and groped from the building. He took time to insert the screws into the ravaged hinges of the rear door, thus fastening the door as it had been before. Then he returned to the boardwalk. But before he headed back to the Seraglio, he took a turn as far as Dryfooting's railroad depot.

The hotel door was locked when he reached it, and his knock brought an outcry from Stumpy. "Name yourself, mister, or I'll blow yore hat off yore head!"

"It's me—Rowdy."

Stumpy was casing his gun with one hand as he swung open the door with the other. "Nothing's stirred since you left," he reported. "But I was playin' safe. I don't trust this hotel any more."

"Then you'll be happy to get out of it," Rowdy said. He fished inside his boot for his money, peeled a couple of bills from the packet of currency and extended these to

Stumpy. "There's a train at the siding right now—a freight with a couple of stock cars and a caboose. It's headed west, so likely it will go through Helena. Get down to the depot right quick. You can buy passage in the caboose from the train crew."

"I ain't lost nobody in Helena," Stumpy said sourly.

"You're going there just the same," Rowdy said. "And when you get there, you're going up to the State Historical Society's library. Griffen's journal is there now, on display likely. Get it and fetch it back here. I'm still playing a hunch, and maybe this will be a wild goose chase. But there's only one way to find out. And, Stumpy, that dinero is for train fare and expenses coming and going. Don't forget that it isn't your birthday—not yet."

Stumpy was easing into his boots which he'd removed. Suddenly he straightened, struck hard by a thought. "But I can't leave town," he wailed. "I gotta be at that official hearing tomorrow morning. I promised Katharine. If I fail that good woman a second time, there ain't gonna be a shred of faith in humanity left in her. Remember what she said about next to a drinkin' man she couldn't stand an undependable galoot? You reckon there's a train out tomorrow afternoon?"

"Stumpy," his partner said firmly, "be on that freight. Pronto. Ever since you landed in that Dryfooting calaboose, it looks to me like you've been teetering on the edge of a cliff. If I have to hog-tie you to keep you from taking a tumble, I'll do it! Mister, get going. I'm only saving you from yourself."

13

JAIL-BREAK!

Rowdy, stretched upon the hotel bed after the reluctant departure of Stumpy Grampis, lay idly reflecting upon the events of the evening, and he found them good. Jake Kelhorn had gotten his twine thoroughly tangled and was in jail now, and the saddle was safe again—or so Rowdy supposed. The last time he'd seen the kak it had been in Nan's arms in the opera house aisle, and the Rimrock Kid had been hovering over the girl, a ready gun in his hand. Likely the Kid had stuck close to Nan ever since. The Kid had fallen hard for the girl sharpshooter, if Rowdy was any judge of signs. Rowdy couldn't blame him for that. But Cupid had apparently traded his arrows for a Gatling gun. Even Stumpy was acting moon-struck, and the remembrance of that made Rowdy sigh. Spring was most definitely in the air.

Beyond the hotel's planking, the town was growing quieter, the blatancy of the saloons diminishing, and Rowdy thought of sleep, but not with enthusiasm. His body ached from the hard pounding Kelhorn had given it, and a sense of loneliness had haunted him ever since Stumpy had left. Rowdy had heard the freight train's whistle all of a half hour ago and knew that it had made its departure. A restlessness had grown in him since, and he swung his legs to the floor and stomped into his boots which he'd discarded. There was always work to be done, and one chore could be handled right now. He wanted a word or two with Nan and her grandfather.

When he came along the hotel hall, he still found light seeping under the door he had earlier identified as belonging to the troupers' room. Voices babbled behind the door, and when Rowdy knocked, Nan admitted him. The room, a replica of Rowdy's, gave into an adjoining one, but both the girl and her grandfather were in this one room at the moment, Nathaniel Faust reclining in a rocker while the Rimrock Kid sat perched upon a chair that had probably been fetched from the second room. Nan's eyes lighted, and she said, "Come in. This seems to be our night for company, but if you don't mind sitting on the edge of the bed—"

"It looks softer than most saddles," Rowdy observed gallantly and crossed the room.

Faust smiled and made an eloquent gesture with one hand. "I'm glad you dropped in, Mr. Dow," he said. "I've wanted to thank you and your partner for your services this evening—especially you. Our young friend, here, has explained some of the circumstances which brought you to our aid. I'm afraid Nan would have fared badly in her defense of the saddle if you hadn't happened along to help her."

Rowdy said, "And just where is the saddle now?"

The Rimrock Kid's white teeth flashed as he grinned. "In the safest place in Dryfooting," he said. "The town banker is a friend of mine; he handles the business end of my wild horse dealings. I got him to open his bank tonight, and the saddle's stowed away in his vault. We haven't seen the last of the Winged-H boys. They won't let Kelhorn roost in the calaboose. And when they make a try at peeling the pokey off him, they may likewise make a play for the saddle. Except for the banker, nobody outside this room knows where the saddle is."

Rowdy glanced at Faust. "Do you intend to be around here for another day or so?"

"Probably," said Faust. "It has occurred to me that I owe you an explanation of sorts. You've proved how you stand. In the jail this morning, you displayed a curiosity regarding the saddle. I told you then that it was valuable to one man only. I'm expecting that man to call upon me and offer to buy the saddle. I'll be here long enough to give him a chance to do so."

"Would that man be Caleb Hackett of the Winged-H?"

Faust started, his hand jerking nervously to his white beard. "How did you know?"

"I didn't," Rowdy admitted with a grin. "Not for sure. It was a shot in the dark. But before you say any more it's only fair to tell you one thing. I'm working for Caleb Hackett. Sort of special agent, you might say. The pay is dubious and the chances for advancement aren't worth a plugged peso, but I've got to admit that I'm learning a lot on the job."

The Rimrock Kid came out of his chair, his dark eyes snapping angrily. "You're working for *Hackett!*"

"That's right as rain," said Rowdy. "That's why I headed for the Winged-H after I visited your camp this afternoon. Does it make a difference?"

"You know blasted well I've got no reason to love the Winged-H," the Kid snapped. "You saw what happened in the Tarantula!"

Rowdy shrugged. It was on his tongue to say that circumstances had indicated that the policies of Caleb Hackett were one thing, the ambitions of his foreman quite another, but he chose to keep silent on that subject. There were yet a few pieces to be fitted into a puzzle before the pattern could be put on display. So he only said, "Keep that checkered shirt of yours on, Kid. You remarked yourself, out at the Winged-H tonight, that it was mighty plain I was no friend of Jake Kelhorn's. That still holds true, even if Jake and I have got the same boss. And I'm here to do business that should please Mr. Faust. I can make an offer for that saddle on behalf of Caleb Hackett. I've got the power to do it. What's your price, Faust?"

"Five thousand dollars," said Nathaniel Faust.

Rowdy whistled. "Pretty steep for an old kak that looks like it will shortly be needing haywire to hold it together!"

"Tennyson Tolbert didn't think so," Faust said.

"Who's shooting in the dark now?" Rowdy asked with a grin. "Yes, I know all about Tennyson Tolbert and the headache he's handed Caleb Hackett. I'm guessing that you know the story too, Faust, otherwise you wouldn't be starting your dicker at such a price. But where's the proof that this saddle you've got is the one Tolbert mentioned in his rime?"

However astonished Nathaniel Faust might have been a few minutes before, he'd completely recovered himself. He spread his hands in that eloquent gesture of his, and he said, "I'm going to trust you with more of the truth than Caleb Hackett would get out of me if he were here. I'm going to trust you because I think you've proved worthy of trust. Once you had the saddle, and you intended returning it to us and told the Rimrock Kid so. You were willing to shoot square. Yes, our saddle is the one that Tolbert dubbed the Devil's Saddle. At least that's what he called it when he shipped it to us from Hamilton. We were playing a Black Hills town when it caught up with us. It had chased us all over the Dakotas."

"I see," Rowdy surmised. "Tolbert was an old friend of yours. Knowing that he was dying, he wanted to do something for you. He'd written Hackett and sent him a queer poem about a Devil's Saddle. Then he'd turned the actual saddle over to you. Also, he'd advised you that Caleb Hackett would be willing to pay high for that saddle. A great man for a joke, friend Tolbert."

"I wouldn't know," Faust said. "Believe me, I never set eyes on Tennyson Tolbert in my life. Neither did my granddaughter. We were absolutely astonished when the saddle arrived, and his letter on the heels of it. He'd apparently spent quite a bit of effort locating us."

Now it was Rowdy's turn to be astonished. "Then why in blazes *did* Tolbert send the saddle to you?"

"He had a reason. He explained it in his letter. That reason was a very personal thing and need not concern us now. Let's call it a family matter. The point is that he felt obligated to us, even though he'd never seen us. Also, he had sensed an opportunity to make Caleb Hackett squirm, and, if Hackett has confided in you, you've likely learned that there was no love lost between Caleb Hackett and Tennyson Tolbert. Tolbert asked us to incorporate the saddle into our act somehow, and to have the billing carry a reference to the Devil's Saddle. Also he asked us to be sure and perform in Dryfooting or its vicinity. He assured us that if we did so, we'd be approached by Caleb Hackett who'd try to buy the saddle from us. It was Tolbert's idea that we should get at least five thousand dollars for it."

Rowdy ran his hand through his hair. Things were coming far too fast for him to coordinate them, and he said, "I don't quite grab where Tolbert expected to get his laugh out of this, but you'd be surprised how generous I am with Caleb Hackett's money." He paused, remembering that he had no real notion as to how much ten percent of Griffen's Gold would be. "You've made a deal, Professor. You'll get at least five thousand dollars for the saddle—maybe more."

Faust's face took on a grim cast. "It will have to be in cash, and it will have to come to me from the hand of Caleb Hackett. Your word is good with me, Dow, but those are the rules of the game. Shall we shake on it?"

"Why not?" said Rowdy and crossed the room and offered his hand. "I'll ride to the Winged-H come morning. Which means I better get some sleep." He swept the room with his eyes. "Good night to all of you."

The Rimrock Kid said, "Good night, *amigo*. There's a lot I don't savvy, and likely it's none of my business. But I can see now why Hackett's had his crew chasing that saddle; he aimed to save himself from shelling out cash. That deal's between the rest of you. But you can tell your boss for me that he'll do better if he looks closer to home for his missing cattle."

"You'll do to ride the river with, Kid," Rowdy said as he stepped toward the door which Nan held open for him. "And I'll have you and Hackett eating off the same plate before I quit this country."

And that was when he heard the roaring of the guns.

Six-shooters were apt to bark at any hour in Dryfooting, but this was no festive smoke let loose by some liquored cowpuncher who'd tilted too many drinks. Several guns were yammering, and not in the direction where most of the saloons were clustered but at the other end of the street where the jail-building sat. And suddenly Rowdy understood. From the moment that Jake Kelhorn had been locked up, Rowdy had known that a play would be made by his confederates to release the man. But here was the audacity of it, and therefore the advantage: the Winged-H was striking this very night and thus gaining an element of surprise.

The Rimrock Kid had grasped the situation too; he came bounding into the hallway, his dark eyes afire with anger. Nan, disappearing into the adjoining room, returned with a rifle in her hands. Rowdy barked, "You stay here, girl! You might be handy at shooting that thing, but it's dodging bullets that will be the job tonight. Professor, keep her here!"

Then he and the Kid were darting down the hall and taking the steps two at a time. They came bursting out upon the boardwalk and peered up the street toward the jail. Dim movements stirred the shadows yonder, gun-flame creased the night, and there was much shouting and cursing. Obviously Catastrophe Kate had been in her office when the attempt had been made at a jail-break, and obviously the sheriff, now forted up in that same office, was giving Kelhorn's friends a lively time of it. The Winged-H was making no attempt at silence; their strategy seemed to be to free Kelhorn by one determined, ruthless rush. And they had picked an hour when most of Dryfooting was fogged with sleep.

Rowdy went forward at a hard run, the Kid at his elbow. But suddenly the Kid was angling away, cutting between two buildings and vanishing into a black void. Rowdy understood. The Kid was circling to get behind the jail and thus to outflank the raiders on one side while Rowdy descended upon them from the other. But Rowdy and the Kid were just sixty seconds too late.

Riders came roaring down the street, three of them abreast, and from their saddles ran ropes to some bouncing thing in the dust. A cell window, bars, frame, and all. Those three had snagged ropes around the bars, and, with concerted heave of the three horses, had torn the window from the side of the building. Now a fourth horse came galloping along, and a fifth, the last one double-burdened, for Jake Kelhorn sat behind the saddle, clutching hard at the man who handled the reins. Rowdy lifted his gun and fired, and, firing, knew that he'd missed.

Bullets began peppering about him, the aim behind them erratic, for those Winged-H men were firing from pitching saddles, but, since a stray bullet can leave a man just as dead as any other kind, Rowdy backed quickly to the boardwalk, hunkered behind a barrel on the porch of a mercantile store, and returned the fire. But not for long. The Winged-H crew, their rescued foreman with them, swirled on down the street and then seemed to vanish. A man materialized from the shadows and came running toward the store, and Rowdy saw that it was the Rimrock Kid.

"They made it, damn them!" the Kid cried. "You saw Kelhorn? Now where in blazes have they gone? Looks like they separated and headed between buildings."

"You'd better get back to the hotel," Rowdy advised. "They might have the nerve to make a play for the saddle too, and they'll suppose it's with Faust and the girl. Me, I'll see how Catastrophe Kate made out."

Mrs. McCandless had made out not so well, thank you. When Rowdy came running to the jail-building after the Kid had darted away in the opposite direction, he found the sheriff standing on the steps, a smoking gun in her hand. She was unwounded physically, but her pride had been scarred. She loosed a litany of profanity that would have made a mule-skinner faint, and out of this medley of plain and fancy cussing Rowdy got the general situation. Her first inkling of the raid had been when horses had whinnied at the far side of the building. Kate had started for the door and been driven back by bullets. A couple of Winged-H hands had stationed themselves in a position to keep her penned up, while the others had literally torn the side out of the building. Somebody, Kate McCandless fervently promised, was going to suffer for this.

"They'll take to the badlands," Rowdy judged. "A posse might cut sign come morning. But we might as well go to sleep as far as tonight is concerned."

He turned and headed back toward the hotel, smarting with a consciousness of defeat. And in this mood he found the Rimrock Kid bearing down upon him at a hard run. Even before the Kid caught his breath and could speak, Rowdy sensed that the full extent of the disaster had not fallen upon Catastrophe Kate. The Kid was almost weeping with rage.

"They got her!" he cried. "They must have had it all

planned to a T, and it only took a couple of them to do it. They came up the back stairs of the hotel and had her and her granddad under guns before either of them could make a move. When they found the saddle wasn't in sight, the men didn't waste time looking for it. They grabbed Nan instead."

Rowdy got a hard grip on the Kid's arm. "They kidnapped Nan?"

"They're going to hold her till Faust gives them the saddle. They said for him to fetch it to the badlands and build a signal fire. Faust told me that much before he headed out to find a horse. He's on his way to the Winged-H, Dow. He said that he'd been crazy to ever think that a man could do business with Caleb Hackett. He was loco mad. He says Caleb Hackett is behind all this. And he swears he'll kill Hackett before the sun rises."

"Come on!" Rowdy shouted and ran toward the livery stable. Not very long ago he'd been reflecting upon the evening and finding it good. In the short span since, everything had changed. Jake Kelhorn held all the cards, and Caleb Hackett, alone and helpless in his ranch-house, was likely to die for what Jake Kelhorn had done.

14

THE HAND OF TENNYSON TOLBERT

Rowdy went out of Dryfooting like a turpentined terrier on a downhill tilt, but he made his ride alone. The Rimrock Kid had gone running back in the general direction of the hotel, and Rowdy, after shouting at him till he'd rubbed his tonsils raw, wasted no more time. At the livery stable Rowdy was told that Nathaniel Faust had rented a

saddle horse in a considerable hurry, asked the way to the
Winged-H and lit out as though the devil were dogging
his heels. The hostler had also mentioned that the great
Professor Marvelo had been carrying a Winchester rifle.
Caleb Hackett, it seemed, was due to take on the perfo-
rated appearance of a Swiss cheese in a very short time.

Therefore Rowdy, likewise renting a saddler so that he
might have a fresh horse beneath him, went beelining into
the badlands with the full knowledge that it was up to
him, and him alone, to keep blood from being spilled
tonight. He'd liked to have had the Rimrock Kid at his
stirrup to point the way, but that love-smitten hunter of
wild horses seemed to have been possessed of an idea of
his own, and Rowdy hadn't been of a mind to comb the
town for the Kid. Rowdy was a bit more familiar with this
badlands country than he'd been when he'd first ridden
into it, and, as he kept his eye peeled for landmarks he'd
noticed when he and the Kid had ridden into town earlier
this evening, he consoled himself with the thought that
Faust, having never covered this trail, could hardly be
making fast progress. But the old magician had something
of a start, and that could make all the difference. Rowdy
worked his quirt with vigor.

Somewhere out here was Jake Kelhorn and his crew,
and with them was Nan Bolton, and Rowdy was mindful
of the possibilities of a bushwhack trap as he rode along.
But Kelhorn's bunch, who might reasonably be expecting
to find a posse on their heels, were likely letting no grass
grow under them. Would they be loping to the ranch?
That would be a fine howdy-you-do, to run headlong into
the whole outfit at the Winged-H! Yet they'd hardly dare
fetch their captive to the spread. Jake Kelhorn was still
trying to palm himself off on his employer as a paragon of
all the virtues, and that meant that Kelhorn would
scarcely be so bold as to bring the kidnapped girl to Hack-

ett's house. Also, Kelhorn would be remembering that Catastrophe Kate, with a posse at her heels, would be having a look in at the ranch just as a matter of routine.

Rowdy was not concerned about Nan's safety. There were a good many reasons why Kelhorn would hesitate to do the girl any real harm, except at some desperate, last-ditch stand. Nan was too valuable as a hostage to be handled with anything but care. No, the Rimrock Kid might be in a sweat because of the girl's predicament, but Rowdy's concern was of another kind. Tonight a man might die, a man who was guiltless so far as the activities of Jake Kelhorn were concerned, and that would be tragedy in itself. And tonight Nathaniel Faust, torn by grief and anger, might bloody his hands, and that, too, would be tragedy. For there was much that Faust didn't understand, and, when the truth came out, the old magician would know regret all of his days.

Come to think of it, there was a great deal that Rowdy, himself, didn't understand. But as he pounded through this weird world of lingering echoes and misshapen rocks, it came to him that a good many people tonight, himself included, were like puppets on strings, dancing to the maneuverings of the dead hand of Tennyson Tolbert. A rare bird, that Tolbert, moving in mysterious fashion his wonders to perform. Now, at last, Rowdy knew how that decrepit looking kak that was labeled the Devil's Saddle had come into the deal. Tolbert, for reasons of his own, had placed in Faust's hands a means of extorting money from Hackett. But the coin that Faust was intent upon dealing in tonight was to be fashioned from hot lead.

More than half-way from the town to the ranch, Rowdy had to rest his horse for a few minutes, and this he did, begrudging the time. The badlands lay ghostly and brooding, bathed by a moth of a moon that seemed to have no heart for its work. Some ominous bird of the night made swift, whirring passage overhead; rocks rattled on the trail to the scurrying of a rodent that never quite showed itself. For a moment Rowdy's heart did a backward somersault with the thought that hoofs had sired that rattling sound, and even when he realized he was mistaken, he experimentally cupped his hands to his mouth and called Faust's name loudly. The echoes caught his voice and mocked him, and Rowdy couldn't repress a shudder. He'd heard of ranges where men got so lonesome they talked to the rocks, but it was a mighty scary matter when the rocks started talking back to a fellow. These badlands . . . !

Plying his quirt again, Rowdy went clattering along the trail, and soon he was into that changed, loam-carpeted land and skirting the maze of canyons where today he'd played a deadly game of hide-and-seek with Kelhorn's men. Yonder, in the distance, loomed the huge, sentinel rock that shadowed the Kid's camp, and Rowdy, glancing toward that isolated landmark, peered more intently, struck by a thought. Then he shook his head, bending his attention to the trail ahead. This was no time for the flight of fancy upon which his thought might have taken him.

The moon was still aloft when he sighted that slight rise where the two-storied Winged-H ranch house perched, and he saw that only one light showed in the building, a wavering light, and this in the upper story. The bedroom of Caleb Hackett, he judged, remembering his one entry into the house, and he kicked a last burst of speed from his cayuse. Soon he was near enough to make out the windmill and tank, and the high crossarm from which the brass dinner bell was suspended. When he reached the ranch-yard gate he found a spent saddler standing with drooping head.

Lighting down, Rowdy looped the reins of his own saddler over a gate post and laid a hand on the dripping flank of the other horse. A man had ridden hard and fast tonight, and that man was Nathaniel Faust. There were only a few horses in the corrals, from the sound of things, and the ranch had that same air of desertion that had marked it in the afternoon. Jake Kelhorn and his men apparently weren't here, but Faust was on hand. Rowdy crossed the yard quickly, mounted the gallery steps and let himself into the house without knocking.

The wide hallway was as dark as the inside of a black cat on a stormy night, and Rowdy went groping gingerly until he found the stairs. He ascended with the same caution, one part of his consciousness screaming for him to hurry, the other reminding him that it wouldn't do to break his neck. He got to the upper hallway, and an open door, the one leading into Hackett's bedroom, let lamplight spill out upon the carpet, and Rowdy was able to move faster. But now he could hear voices—the voices of two men—and relief turned Rowdy's knees rubbery. For one of those voices belonged to Caleb Hackett—blatant proof that the man was still alive.

"Of course I don't know you," Hackett was saying. "Why should I? When you turned up that lamp and shone it in my face, I thought you were something left over from a nightmare I'd been having. What's your business, mister? And what makes it so important that you have to come busting into a man's house in the middle of the night?"

"My name," he was told, "is Nathaniel Faust."

And this was the means by which Rowdy discovered that at the last he'd only been a minute or two behind the magician. Faust had just nicely gotten into the house and found the man he was seeking, a feat which had probably taken a little time. And now Faust had identified himself. The sudden silence that fell was electrifying; it was compounded of astonishment and perhaps of fear, yet it left Rowdy in no such great hurry as he had been. Faust's voice had been calm and soft; whatever anger had driven the magician on his wild ride from Dryfooting had congealed to ice; and there'd be no gun-play. Not yet. And Rowdy, who'd intended to come barging into that bedroom to disarm Faust as quickly as possible, stayed his hand now, gliding silently along the far wall of the hallway until he could see into the room. For every instinct that Rowdy possessed whispered that what was to be said next was going to be worth listening to.

From where he paused, he could look through the doorway, and if either man had glanced his way they would have seen him, too. But both oldsters were far too intent upon each other to have even a subconscious inkling of Rowdy's presence. Caleb Hackett was exactly as Rowdy had last seen him, nightgown-clad and lost in the immensity of his bed. Nathaniel Faust stood at the foot of that bed, a lamp held in his left hand, a rifle crooked carelessly under his right arm. The dramatist in Faust was obviously giving him a fine appreciation of this moment, for Caleb Hackett was staring as a man stares who sees the unbelievable. And Hackett broke that long, quivering silence to say, whisperingly, "Nathaniel Faust! *Nat Faust—!*"

"Not young Nat," Faust said. "He's dead. So is Esmerelda. But I was Nat's father, and I'm judging that you're seeing his ghost in my face. You didn't like my boy, did you, Hackett? You hated him because your daughter preferred to run away and starve with him than to stay here and listen to your bitter tongue. But I didn't come to talk about Nat. Where is she, Hackett?"

"*She—?*" Hackett said hollowly. "Who do you mean?"

"Nan," Faust said. "Your granddaughter and mine. Nat and Esmerelda's girl."

Hackett twitched violently. "*Granddaughter!* I never knew they had a child. I never knew. I learned that Esmerelda was dead. That was years ago. I looked her up, Faust. I looked her up to help her. Whatever else you think of me, you've got to believe that. Yes, I hated Nat, and he hated me, and I suppose he got you to hate me, too. But you can't blame me, Faust. Esmerelda was all I had. It hurt a heap to see her take off with a young whippersnapper who made a poor living barnstorming through the country with a juggling act. I had plans for Esmerelda. So they had a child! I never knew . . ."

Faust tipped back his fine head and laughed, and there was an edge of hysteria to the sound. "I raised Nan," he said. "We were a theatrical family, and I took her into my act when she was only a child. And I helped train her, years later, when she started shaping up an act of her own. Nan Bolton is her stage name. Now I can understand one thing. I didn't think that even *you* would be so heartless as to have your crew carry off your own granddaughter just to lay your hands on that saddle. But you didn't know that Nan Bolton was Nan Faust. Can you understand why I'm laughing, Hackett?"

Hackett said, "The things I *can't* understand would fill a fat book. What's this talk about my crew, and the saddle? And Nan? For heaven's sake, man, don't stand there behaving like this was a stage performance! Tell me what you're driving at!"

"Tennyson Tolbert sent us the saddle," Faust said. "Also, he sent us a letter telling us to work the saddle into our act and to bill it as the Devil's Saddle. He said that if we played Dryfooting, you'd come running and try to buy the saddle from us. Tolbert was always mighty fond of Esmerelda; he told me so in his letter. Without ever having walked into Nan's life or mine, he'd been keeping track, the best he could, of Nan. Dying, he wanted to do something for Esmerelda's girl, and at the same time he wanted to plague you. He frankly admitted that. He'd get

a last laugh out of thinking of you having to pay through
the nose for that saddle—and the superb irony was that
you were going to have to be paying me—*me*, the father
of Nat Faust, the boy you despised!"

Out in the hall, Rowdy sucked in his breath. Now he
knew the personal part of that letter Tolbert had sent Nathaniel Faust. But, more than that, he was getting a new
insight into the character of Tennyson Tolbert. Why hadn't
the old prospector, anxious to help Esmerelda's daughter,
given Nan the key to Griffen's Gold and forgotten Caleb
Hackett altogether? Was it because Tolbert, a square-
shooter at heart, had had to remember that it had been
Caleb Hackett who'd grubstaked him?

"I've looked that saddle over carefully," Faust was saying. "I believe it's worthless and that Tolbert intended
that I should swindle you. Just why he was so sure that
you'd pay some wild amount for the saddle, I don't know.
But I'll admit that I intended to get the money from you,
if you were foolish enough to pay it. That was to be for
Nan's sake. We haven't had an easy life, Hackett. You
don't know what it is to jump from town to town the
cheapest way, saving every cent for costumes and for a
stagecoach of our own. You've never lived in theatrical
hotels and sat up half a night writing letters to theaters in
towns ahead, hoping to get booking and depending on
your mail from one week to the next to know whether
you're going to be eating in the future. Yes, I'd have swin-
dled you with no more compunction than I'd have had
against setting my heel on the head of a snake. But you're
still as tight-fisted and grasping as you were when you
turned your own daughter out without a cent. You weren't
willing to *buy* the saddle from me. You sent your crew to
steal it, and, failing in that, they've kidnapped Nan and
are holding her hostage in return for the saddle."

A dry, inhuman sound burst from the throat of Caleb

Hackett, but Faust gave him no time to force speech. "I rode here tonight for one reason," Faust said. "To make you tell me where Kelhorn has taken Nan. But perhaps you don't even know. I had a look in your barn and bunkhouse before I came up here, and the only person I could find was an unconscious Mexican out in the yard. But still you get a chance to talk. Where is she, Hackett? Tell me, or I'm driving a bullet through your stingy, wretched heart!"

Hackett kicked his blankets aside. "Where's my pants?" he howled. "There's been a heap going on here that I haven't known about, but I'm beginning to savvy why Kelhorn kept selling me on the notion that I was sick and had to stay in bed. Faust, I didn't even know you were on earth, let alone within a million miles of here. And I didn't know you had a saddle that Tennyson Tolbert sent you, so I couldn't have been making a play for that saddle. Jake Kelhorn has been acting on his own, and you and me are going to smoke him out and take that girl away from him. Right now!"

Nathaniel Faust took a backward step, and the rifle came level in his hands and was lined on Hackett's chest. "Stay where you are!" Faust thundered. "Do you think you can bluff me with that kind of talk? Stay where you are—and get ready to take the medicine you've been needing for a long time! Do you hear?"

Rowdy took two lunging steps forward and framed himself in the doorway. "Put down that rifle, Professor," he said. "Hackett likely needs shooting just on general principles, but you've got him all wrong this time. He's been telling it straight. He doesn't know any more about what Kelhorn's been doing than an antelope knows about arithmetic. You can't shoot a man for being stupid."

15

There was one thing about spending an evening at the theater, Rowdy decided; it certainly taught a man how to make a dramatic entry. Standing here in the doorway, he savored the utter astonishment of both Faust and Hackett. According to the best tradition of such playwrights as Rowdy had been exposed to, both of these oldsters should now come forward and wring his hand, thanking him humbly for having prevented a tragedy. Hackett should be the most grateful, and that crusty old codger should undergo a complete reversal of character, pledging himself to an unselfish life and endowing Rowdy with a half-interest in his ranch to prove his sincerity. All that would be then needed to complete the scene would be a descending curtain, some soft and appropriate music, and the applause of the audience.

But Caleb Hackett was apparently no patron of the drama. The oldster's astonishment changed to anger, and, his eyes fixed on Rowdy, he said, "Stupid, am I! A fine fix you got me into! Said you knew the man who had the Devil's Saddle, didn't you? Said you'd act as my agent and buy that saddle. Why in blazes didn't you do it? No, you left me to be woke up in the middle of the night with a rifle poked at my brisket! A fine mess you made of everything!"

And Faust, that man who'd been saved from making a grave error? Was he brimming with gratitude? Faust swung the rifle, lining it on Rowdy, and the old trouper said, "You admitted you were Hackett's agent, Dow. You're still doing his work, I see. But I'm not going to let you stand between him and me. You're no friend of Jake

Kelhorn's; I know that. But I'm wondering now just what lonewolf sort of hand you're playing!"

The time had come, Rowdy decided wearily, for a man to talk—and talk fast. Cards held close to his vest had seemed like slick strategy before, but those cards didn't make a man's vest bullet-proof. He began with the letter he'd received from Caleb Hackett; he told of his and Stumpy's coming to the badlands, and he spared no incident and withheld no fact in giving a complete account of all that had happened since. He made it sound sincere, for, as he talked, Nathaniel Faust's rifle gradually sagged, but, when the tale was told, Caleb Hackett was angrier than ever.

"Why didn't you tell me the truth about Jake before?" Hackett demanded. "You knew it when you first came here. All you told me was to quit taking the medicine Kelhorn was fetching. Dow, you ain't got any more brains than gawd gave little gophers." He glared around wildly. "Where's my pants? I'm riding!"

"After the saddle?" Faust asked softly. "Now I understand what makes it valuable. The key to Griffen's Gold, eh?"

"No, you goat-whiskered old die-hard!" Hackett roared. "I'm riding after Jake Kelhorn. I'm taking our girl away from him, and then I'm chasing him and his crew till their pockets are dipping sand!"

Faust's seamed face softened with a smile. "There's a heart in you," he conceded. "There's a heart in you, after all."

Hackett's own face softened. "My pride stood between me and Esmerelda," he said. "I could have had my daughter, and a son-in-law as well, but I was too confounded stubborn. All my pride got me was a lot of lonely years. If you poisoned Nan against me, Faust, you had a right to do it. But I'm gonna prove to her that her other granddad ain't such a bad galoot."

"You're going to stay in that bed," Rowdy said firmly. "Till morning." He crossed the room and seated himself on the edge of the bed and began tugging at a boot. "Move over and make a little room for me and the Professor. Pile in, Faust. We all need rest. We couldn't do anything tonight but fall over rocks. Morning will give us a chance to cut sign on Jake Kelhorn."

Hackett looked for a moment as though he were going to explode, and then he grinned. "That's good judgment," he conceded. "Maybe you *are* worth your salt, Dow. Mind you, I ain't saying that I'm sure. We'll ride, come morning."

The question was not which of the three snored, but who snored the loudest. They awoke with sunlight streaming through the bedroom window, and they came downstairs to the kitchen where Caleb Hackett got coffee boiling while Rowdy poked through a cupboard and found some bacon. Hackett, dressed in range garb, proved to be steady of step, and Rowdy judged that the means by which Kelhorn had kept his employer bedfast had been mostly by suggestion. They were eating when a face was pressed fleetingly against the kitchen window. It didn't make the kind of picture a man would care to frame and hang over his fireplace, and Rowdy came to his feet so suddenly he almost overturned the table.

"Pablo Diablo!" he ejaculated.

When Rowdy got to the gallery, Pablo was rounding the house aboard a horse, bending low over the saddlehorn and quirting hard. Rowdy got his gun into his hand and tilted it, then withheld his fire, struck by an idea. Turning back into the house, he swiftly ran up the stairs, entered Hackett's bedroom and peered from the window. Here he had a good view of the Mexican as Pablo Diablo streaked away toward the southeast, and he watched the fellow until Pablo had disappeared. Whereupon Rowdy returned to the kitchen.

"Get him?" Hackett demanded.

"I let him go," Rowdy said. "Too bad that we forgot all about him, but Faust said that the Mex was unconscious last night. The Rimrock Kid must have fetched him a mighty powerful clout. Yesterday, when I first called here, Pablo seemed to know exactly where to find Kelhorn. I'm judging that he's heading for Kelhorn again. By letting him go, I let him point the way. He's heading straight for that canyon maze where Kelhorn's boys played tag with me."

"And we'll be riding the same direction," Hackett declared, pushing back his plate.

Within a few minutes the three were astride saddlers and riding away from the ranch. Hackett had equipped himself with a huge horse pistol of ancient vintage and doubtful potentialities, and Faust still packed the Winchester which, Rowdy judged, was one of Nan's collection. They beelined toward the deeper badlands, that canyon maze of which Rowdy had no entrancing memories, and Rowdy urged caution rather than haste. The idea was to overtake Kelhorn—but not to walk into his brawny arms. They had scarcely gotten into the first of the canyons when they heard the *clip-clop* of shod hoofs upon rock; and Rowdy's hand dropped instinctively to his holster. But it was a lone horseman who rode around a turn and into their view, and that horseman was the Rimrock Kid.

"Over here, Kid," Rowdy called from the shadow of a huge rock where the trio had hidden themselves at the first sound of hoofs.

The wild horse hunter looked like he needed a good

night's sleep; his ready grin was not in evidence, his lips were drawn tight, and he looked even grimmer when his eyes lighted on Caleb Hackett. Rowdy said hastily, "Hackett's on our side, Kid. Believe it or not, he's Nan's grandpappy too, but that's a long story and we'll tell you about it later."

Hackett said, "Kelhorn had me believing you were rustling my cattle, Kid. I gave orders to shoot you on sight or to hang you from the handiest tree, if the boys had the time to spare. That's the old-fashioned way of taking care of rustlers. I reckon Kelhorn had me fooled a heap. You willing to let bygones be bygones?"

When Rowdy had announced that Hackett was kin to Nan, the Kid had looked as though a stiff breeze would have brushed him out of his saddle. Now the Kid said, "The only thing that counts with me today is finding Nan. I'm on my way to build a signal fire. I reckon the best place would be atop that big rock where I have my camp."

Rowdy's eyes dropped to the saddle the Kid was sitting, and that saddle was all too familiar. "So you fetched the kak," Rowdy observed.

"I got it last night," the Kid said. "I had to get my banker friend out of bed, and that's where I was heading when I left you. Yes, I fetched the saddle. I spent all night trying to find Kelhorn and make the swap. To hell with the saddle. He can have it, and fifty like it, if he'll turn Nan loose like he promised."

"My guess is that we're mighty close to Kelhorn right now," Rowdy said. "Pablo Diablo headed this way, and Pablo wasn't guessing where he was going. Kid, you know these canyons better than most. Is there one that's kind of out of the way and runs long and wide but pinches together tight at both ends?"

The Kid's dark eyes widened. "There's a couple like that, and one's not far from here. How did you know?"

Rowdy sighed, remembering the governor's pardon that he carried and remembering also the older days that had ended with the signing of that pardon. "I knew a cattle rustler once," he said. "So I know the sort of place rustlers would want so they could hold stolen beef while they changed the brands. It would have to be big enough to accommodate them, out of the way and hard to find, pinched tight at the ends so it would be easy to guard, and it would have to have a back door as well as a front so the boys could hit the grit if a big posse showed up."

"Follow me," the Kid said with renewed enthusiasm. "I'll take you to the place."

"Let's have a look at it from the rim," Rowdy advised.

They went single-file then, following a trail that would have tied a snake into knots, and often they had to dismount and lead their horses. They climbed, always, and an hour passed, and another, and the sun stood nearly at noon when the Kid's raised hand cautioned silence. "We'll have to go ahead on foot," he said. "Quiet now. We're almost there."

But Rowdy didn't need to be told. He'd already heard the faint bawling of cattle.

Not many minutes later the four were stretched flat on their stomachs and peering over a canyon's rim; and below them spread quite a view. There was a shack of sorts on the canyon's floor, a crude structure crowded against the far wall, and there were corrals, too, and in them were cattle. A smaller corral held horses, and these, Rowdy knew, were the unbranded cayuses the Winged-H crew had ridden the day they'd attacked Faust's fancy stagecoach. This, then, was Kelhorn's hideout. Men, made tiny by distance, lounged about the shack, and suddenly the Kid, at Rowdy's elbow, was sucking in his breath hard, for

Nan had appeared in the doorway of the shack and then disappeared again.

"This is it!" the Kid whispered. "Here's where they've been hazing Winged-H beef, and maybe a few other brands as well. I reckon they drive the stuff north to the Missouri, once the worked-over brands are healed. Seven of them, and four—two of us."

Rowdy knew why the Kid had corrected himself, for the Kid's thought was Rowdy's own. Caleb Hackett and Nathaniel Faust had a stake here, but both were old men and doubtless wouldn't be as handy in a fight as they'd like to suppose. Rowdy said, "The last time I saw Catastrophe Kate she was hopping mad. Likely she'll be along with a big posse this morning. If we could join up with her, we could sweep that canyon like a new broom."

The Kid groaned. "No good. I went to Kate last night before I left town. I begged her to promise not to take a posse out until I gave her the sign. The only thing that mattered to me was getting Nan back, and I intended to swap off the saddle. A posse might have sent Kelhorn running. I didn't want to risk that. When I laid the whole deal before Kate, she promised to hold her horses. She'll keep that promise. We can't count on help from town showing up."

"Kelhorn doesn't know that," Rowdy said thoughtfully. "And Kelhorn is likewise figuring that a posse wouldn't stand one chance in a hundred of stumbling onto this place. I wouldn't have headed here myself if Pablo hadn't given me an idea and I'd tied it together with the fact that Kelhorn must be doing the rustling that you were being blamed for. Kelhorn wanted you dead so he could report to his boss that he'd done his job. After that Kelhorn would have found somebody else to blame the rustling on. But we don't give a whoop about that. Not today. It goes against my grain to think of turning that saddle over to

Kelhorn, whether the saddle's worth anything or not. Mister, a posse is going to pay Kelhorn a surprise visit pronto. And it's going to be such a surprise that I'm counting on him lighting out too fast to bother dragging Nan along with him!"

"You mean I'm to head to town and tell Catastrophe Kate that it's okay to organize a posse?"

Rowdy shook his head. "That would take too long. Nope, *I'm* going to be the posse—a one-man posse. Have you got a dozen or so wild horses corraled near your camp? Some stuff that's been gentled down enough that I can herd 'em along?"

"Why, yes I have," the Kid said.

"Then let's be going after those broomtails. I'll show you what I mean."

The Kid gave him a long, thoughtful look. "I went off half-cocked last night," the Kid admitted. "I know that now. My first mistake was in hog-tying the sheriff with a promise. My second was in lighting out in the dark to try and find Kelhorn. I'm putting my chips on you, Rowdy, and letting you name the play."

"Come on," said Rowdy. "Get us to your camp by the shortest way."

But even the shortest way took time in these badlands. They had to sacrifice haste for silence until they were beyond earshot of Kelhorn's hideout, and after that they had to find their way out of the canyon maze. It was early afternoon when they looked across an open space to that huge sentinel rock which shadowed the Kid's camp, but it wasn't long after that till they'd skirted the rock and were beyond the camp. Here was another canyon maze, and the Kid had fashioned a natural corral out of one of these canyons by blocking its entrance. Inside were a dozen horses, a mixture of colors, and some had matted manes and long, dragging tails. These were the products of the

Kid's sweat—wild horses combed diligently out of the badlands and broken for saddle.

"A fine-looking bunch of oreanas," Rowdy commented.

"The older stuff goes to packing plants for chicken feed," the Kid explained. "The wildest hammerheads make bucking horses for shows, but this stuff has been gentled down. Reckon some of it ends up as saddle stock, and some is sold to the British army. My dealers write that the British buy 'em up for their cavalry."

Rowdy said, "You're going to lose this bunch on a gamble, old son. Here's the idea. We'll leave Hackett and Faust here—" He heard the wild rumble that rose in Caleb Hackett's chest, and he said, "No argument now! Everybody has his place in this scheme, and yours is here. You and Faust will climb atop that sentinel rock and watch for the Kid's return. Him and me will be hazing these broomtails back to the other canyons. When we get near Kelhorn's hideout, I'm riding on in, stampeding these horses ahead of me. I'll do some shouting and some shooting, and Kelhorn's crew will think that a big bunch of riders are a-roaring down on them. I'm banking that Kelhorn won't take time to force Nan into a saddle, especially since she'll probably fight him, figuring that help has come."

"And I'll be right at your side," the Kid said.

"No you won't," Rowdy countered. "Once I go in, I'm going right on through, the idea being to scatter Kelhorn's outfit into the far canyons. I'll keep 'em fooled as long as I can, and, in the meantime, you'll be getting hold of Nan, if they leave her behind. Your chore, Kid, will be to see that she gets safely to this camp. Faust and Hackett will be here, atop the rock, ready to cover you in case part of our scheme goes wrong and you've got Kelhorn on your trail. Everybody got the idea straight?"

Faust smiled gently. "You're afraid we old fellows will

be underfoot at a time when you couldn't risk that. I'm an old man, and I know it. Hackett's an old man, too, but nobody's convinced him of it yet. We'll be here, Dow. Good luck to you."

Hackett began spluttering, but Rowdy pulled the Winged-H owner's floppy sombrero down over his eyes. "You said you'd tie no strings on me," Rowdy reminded him. "I'm dishing out the orders today. Get up on that rock, mister."

The Kid was tearing away the heaped brush with which he'd blocked the entrance to his canyon corral. Rowdy and he rode inside, pocketed the horses and pushed them out through the unblocked opening. They got them headed at a trot in the direction of the Winged-H, and, as they skirted the sentinel rock again, Rowdy saw the two oldsters laboriously climbing upward.

Rowdy gave them a wave of his hand, and after that he concentrated on keeping those dozen horses bunched. They'd been tamed down until they could be handled, but they were getting a sniff of freedom, and the chore was to keep them from developing ideas of their own. But the Kid was a mighty good hand with horses; he'd worked with them so long that apparently he'd learned to think like one, and they proceeded without any incident that might have made a man want to throw his hat on the ground and stomp on it. Once they were into that canyon maze that was within the confines of the Winged-H, Rowdy let the Kid do the guiding, and there finally came a moment when the Kid paused, held up his hand and said, "Here we are."

Yonder was a long, narrow slot, a crevice in the rocks and Rowdy knew then that this was the entrance to the canyon they'd scanned from a high rim. Rowdy grinned, gave his belt a hitch, and said, "Give me a few minutes head start. And hope for luck."

Then he was spurring his mount and snapping at the flanks of the drag horses with his quirt, and suddenly the whole dozen were bolting forward, their hoofs raising a bedlam on the rocky floor. And after them went Rowdy, whooping and hollering and firing his gun. The trail funneled down into the crevice, and, with the walls towering above him, Rowdy shouted, *"Give 'em hell, men! Shoot down every last son if they make a stand!"* Echoes caught his voice and made it twenty voices, and the thunder of hoofs was a din in his ears.

He thought fleetingly of Stumpy. That old hellion would be a good hand to have along at a time like this. Stumpy liked this kind of carrying-on.

16

THAT STRAY LAMB STUMPY

But Stumpy Grampis, that arrant wayfarer, was tending to other matters. Stumpy had gone grumblingly from the Seraglio the night before with explicit instructions from Rowdy to buy passage on a certain freight train and to do a certain chore at the State Historical Library in Helena. Another time Stumpy might have preened himself on the responsibility thus placed on his slight shoulders, but Stumpy was remembering that Catastrophe Kate would be expecting him at a hearing the next morning and that he was going to be conspicuous by his absence. A fine way to treat a lady! Rowdy didn't have any more chivalry to him than you'd find in a barrel of rattlesnakes!

Thus Stumpy had marched along muttering under his breath, but, at the first splash of light falling from a saloon window, he'd paused and had a look at the currency Rowdy had thrust into his hand. It wasn't a sum calculated to set a man up in business on a lavish scale; in fact it would hardly cover passage coming and going, plus a couple of meals in Helena. "Don't forget that it isn't your birthday . . ." Rowdy had admonished him. A fine chance there was to squeeze a drink out of that fund! But Stumpy's eyes narrowed thoughtfully. There were more ways of killing a cat than stuffing it full of gunpowder and using its tail for a fuse. A corner cut here and there on expenses could make a surplus that might be expended pleasantly. A penny saved was a penny earned, some ancient coot had said.

Stumpy looked, longingly inside the saloon, remembered Catastrophe Kate's attitude toward drinking, and forced himself onward. No, by grab! He was a man who could tussle with temptation and throw it three falls out of five! Besides, the train was making a rumpus down by the depot, and he'd better hurry. But if he could get free passage aboard that train, he'd be a few dollars ahead when he hit Helena. After all, a man was entitled to some compensation for barging around in the middle of the night like a confounded hooty-owl.

Bow-legging to the railroad siding, Stumpy found the freight which Rowdy had mentioned. This wasn't the season of heavy cattle shipments—they would be made in the fall—and Stumpy judged that the penned, bawling beef inside the stock cars were on their way to some packing plant, probably in Seattle, to fill a special order. He was peering into one of the cars and considering climbing to its roof, weighing the prospects of a cold, windy ride against the money that would thus be saved, and the pleasures that would accrue from it, when a man loomed up out of the darkness. The man wore a wide sombrero and a ragged slicker, and he carried a pole in his hand. This fellow's function, Stumpy knew, was to work that prod pole between the slats of the stock cars and violently as-

sist fallen critters to their feet. The man regarded Stumpy
belligerently.

"Well?" the fellow challenged. "What do you think
you're doing?"

"I was just lookin' for Emily," Stumpy said mournfully.

"Emily—?"

Now Stumpy was taking a chance that this man was not
a hand from one of the ranches that was shipping these
cattle but was instead some stray cowboy who was working train passage by taking on the job of tending cattle,
helping unload and reload them at each feeding point and
inspecting cars at every stop to make sure that no critters
had fallen and might be trampled. If this were the case,
the man would be in no position to challenge a story
which Stumpy had just formulated. Stumpy cleared his
throat.

"Emily's a critter that I personally raised from a calf,"
he explained. "Me, I ride for the spread that owned her,
and I've been trailing this train ever since Emily was put
aboard. You see, it was me who fust found Emily, a little,
shivering calf, one raw spring day not so many seasons
ago, and I sorta supervised the rearing of her. Do yuh
know, she used to stand outside the bunkhouse window,
next to where I slept, and bawl her heart out. It pains me
to think that Emily's on her way to be turned into beef-
steaks."

"If you think you're gonna take a critter off this train—"
the cowpoke began darkly.

Stumpy raised an appeasing hand. "That ain't the idea,
pardner. Me, I know that Emily's got to go the way of all
flesh. That's life, and it's a thorny road we all tread—cow
critters and humans alike. But I shore wish I could ride a
piece with Emily. It would comfort her just to feel that I
was near. I reckon she could go to the butcher *smilin'* if
she knew I hadn't forsaken her complete. Pardner, do you

reckon you've got room in the caboose for a gent my size?"

The cowpoke pondered this, stroking his chin thoughtfully until Stumpy was afraid he'd pull his jaw to a point. Then: "Come along," the fellow said. "We'll pack you a ways."

"I knew you was a sympathetic soul," Stumpy said joyfully. "I knew you'd believe it if I told you the whole truth about me and Emily!"

His benefactor, who'd started toward the caboose, turned on his heel. "Look," he said. "That yarn about you and your calf is the biggest, fattest lie I've heard in a month of Sundays. But the story alone is worth a ride on this rattler. Pile aboard."

The caboose was warm and lamp-lighted, and there were a couple more stock-tenders inside it, and the train's brakeman as well. To this man of authority, Stumpy's newfound friend said, "This jigger earned himself a lift," and Stumpy seated himself on the edge of a bunk. Couplings jerked, and the train was shortly on its way westward. Stumpy's eyes grew heavy-lidded, but he supposed it would be impolite to just fall asleep under the circumstances. He lay back upon the bunk, determined merely to rest for a moment, and the train, gathering speed, clacked monotonously over the rails. It seemed to be beating out a refrain: "Take it easy . . . take it easy . . . take it easy . . . takeiteasy . . . takeiteasy . . ." Stumpy did. He fell asleep . . .

Dawn light awoke him, streaming through the caboose's window, and Stumpy's first wild reflection was that maybe he'd slept for a couple of days and was now half-way across the state of Washington. The train had stopped; the others had left the caboose, and Stumpy, stumbling frantically outside, drew in his breath in sharp relief. Yonder reared the high, familiar outline of Mount

Helena, and beneath it sprawled Montana's capital city. It just went to show you that if a man lived right, luck played with him.

The early morning held a chill that would have made a set of false teeth chatter in a drawer. Stumpy struck off afoot, warmed himself by walking, and was soon into Helena's tortuous main street, that thoroughfare which follows the mindless meanderings of Last Chance Gulch. An aroma of coffee and a rattle of dishes came from an all-night beanery, and into this establishment Stumpy turned to perch himself upon a stool and do away with a breakfast. Wiping the egg from his down-tilted mustache and paying for the food, he reflected that he was now money ahead to the tune of what it might have cost him to ride here from Dryfooting. Now if there was a saloon open at this hour . . .

But, no. First a man did his work, and thus he earned his fun. That was an admonition handed down to Stumpy by his dear, departed father, and, though the old man's work had been helping himself to other people's horses and his reward an air-dance from the limb of a cottonwood, Stumpy still believed in adhering to this advice. There was that matter of getting Griffen's journal from the State Historical Library. With a sigh, Stumpy headed for the newly built capitol where the library was housed.

Now Helena, like Rome, is a city built upon hills, and of Helena an obscure bard once wrote an ode which began: "Here's to Helena, what a town! Half the streets are upside down . . ." Stumpy, toiling up thoroughfares which were tilted straight to the sky was inclined to believe that here was no hyperbole, and he began to wish that he'd hired a hack. But that would be squandering money foolishly. The way leveled out before he reached the capitol, and though he was still panting when he came inside that domed structure he sounded less like an outmoded steam engine. His bootheels echoing hollowly on the handsome floor, he sought out the historical library. There were more doors than a man could count, and it seemed incredible that they all led somewhere. Once Stumpy leaped sideways, frantically grabbing at his gun, but it was only a stuffed buffalo that had scared him, the creature leering at him with glassy eyes from a shadowy corner.

Dang it all, a building this size got on a man's nerves!

The historical library was open and empty of visitors when Stumpy found it. Within the doorway, Stumpy paused in slack-jawed amazement. There must have been at least a trillion books inside the establishment, and there were paintings upon the walls of various dignitaries who had contributed to fashioning Montana into a state, and there were glass display cases, a great many of them. Behind a desk presided a tall, cadaverous man who looked like an exiled duke, and him Stumpy approached with mingled feelings. Likely this was the governor of Montana, and a proper show of humility was probably called for, but, by grab, Stumpy had never clawed off his hat for any man, and he wasn't starting now.

"You the head ramrod hereabouts?" Stumpy asked.

Mr. Bones regarded him with bored indifference. "I'm the janitor," he said. "The librarian ain't showed up yet this morning."

"Me," said Stumpy, "I'm a scholar. A notorious scholar. I'm looking for a journal that some jasper named Griffen wrote in the early days."

"Exhibits are all in the cases," the janitor said with a wave of his hand. "They're catalogued and carded. You can read, can't you? Journals are in that case, yonder."

Stumpy moved to the indicated case. There were a great number of journals, and all had little, white, neatly printed cards beside them. Stumpy let his eyes rove over

these and suddenly drew in his breath. There, large as
life, was Griffen's journal, and no mistake about it. The
card even said that it was loaned by courtesy of *The
Dryfooting Extra.*

Stumpy could have touched that journal if it hadn't
been for the glass enclosing it. So near, and yet so far. But
Stumpy's alert eye had readily detected an astonishing
fact. The case wasn't even locked! Not understanding that
the exhibits were open to the perusal of scholars, he wondered what was the matter with these library folks. Why,
they were practically asking to be robbed! Stumpy gave a
hasty glance over his shoulder, seeking out the lean
janitor. The man was listlessly sweeping in a far corner,
his back to Stumpy. Less than a minute later Stumpy had
the case opened, and one horny hand had closed over
Griffen's journal and the document had disappeared inside his shirt front.

Stumpy strolled out of the place whistling tunelessly,
but it was disappointment rather than elation that puckered his lips. He'd hoped for better luck here. Now if
there'd been a little opposition to this project and he'd
had to shoot his way out of the capitol, what a story that
would have made to carry back to Rowdy! A plague on
these city folks with their soft and careless ways. They
didn't give a man a chance to get any fun out of living.

The morning was still new, and Stumpy was footloose
and fancy free. He toiled back to the railroad yards, made
some discreet inquiries and learned that a freight would
be heading eastward early that evening. That left the balance of the day to be spent—not to mention certain funds.
A story comparable to the Emily classic could insure free
passage back to the badlands, and Stumpy entered into
his calculations the sum that would thus be saved. Now if
there was a saloon with the proper atmosphere . . .
Rowdy's admonition and the remembrance of Catastrophe

Kate came back to him, but it was not entirely conscience that directed Stumpy's footsteps past the first three saloons. It was a little early to find a saloon anything but a lonely place, and Stumpy, gregarious fellow, craved company to spice his refreshments. If only there were a friend he might visit meanwhile . . .

Yonder loomed the faded shingle of Hop Gow, dealer in jade and tea.

Stumpy had been ambling southward along Last Chance Gulch, and now he was to where the city of Helena had had its beginning, a section of decrepit houses and deserted prospect holes. Here the Chinese had their warrens, for the Chinese were among Helena's first citizens; they had come to gopher under the sides of the mountains and they'd stayed to wrest a living in other ways. Here were laundries and chop-suey establishments, and institutions of the kind Hop Gow ran. And Hop Gow was a name known to Stumpy Grampis, for they had met in the past. Jade and tea might be Hop Gow's advertised products, but he had a substantial sideline as well. Immigration quotas might limit the number of Chinese who could legally enter the United States each year, but such restrictions didn't exist in Canada, not so many miles away. Hop Gow assisted his countrymen across the border and found places for them in the States. This service, of course, was not rendered as a charity.

Here then was a friend whom Stumpy might visit for an hour or so, and he stepped inside Hop Gow's establishment joyfully. Hop Gow himself presided behind a counter, a fat, moon-faced Chinese dressed in a padded robe that made him look even paunchier than he was. His slitted eyes lighted at sight of Stumpy, and his bland, yellow face grew a broad grin. "Stumpy Glampis!" he cried in a high, shrill voice. "You sight for sore nose!"

"You old slant-eyed son o' sin!" Stumpy chortled, his hand extended. "Put 'er there!"

"You lookee mighty fine."

"You'll do till a fatter turkey comes along, yourself."

"How your fliend Lowdy Dow?" Hop Gow inquired politely. "Him in jail some more?"

"Rowdy's finer'n frawg feathers. He sent me down to Helena to do a job that was a little too big for him to handle. He'll be plumb pleased to hear that I ran into you."

Hop Gow recalled his duties as a host. "You likee lice wine?"

"*Lice* wine—?" Stumpy scowled. "Oh, you mean *rice* wine. Why not, pard? Why not?"

Hop Gow tucked his fat hands into voluminous sleeves, padded around the counter on slippered feet, and led the way through a curtained doorway. His shop was dingy and bare, but the room into which Stumpy was ushered was of another world, a resplendent place of teakwood furnishings and multi-colored lanterns. Here a young Chinese, clad in the conventional black alpaca, squatted behind a low table, listlessly thumbing a deck of cards. Hop Gow, by way of introduction, said, "This Wong Duck. Him new to 'Melica. Wong Duck, you savvy Stumpy Glampis? Him velly fine fellah."

Wong Duck, most obviously one of those perambulating products in which Hop Gow dealt, arose and bowed until his forehead almost touched the table top. "Please t' meet," said Wong Duck.

"Him don't speak velly good 'Melican," Hop Gow apologized. "Him trying to learn 'Melican ways."

"You likee play cards?" Wong Duck volunteered hospitably.

"Wa-al now—" Stumpy began, then changed his mind.

Why not? Here was as good a way as any to put in an hour or so.

"You savvy fan-tan?"

"Shore I savvy fan-tan," said Stumpy, and the devil was whispering in his ear. "But I savvy poker better. Poker's the royal game of America, Wong Duck. If you're going to catch onto our ways, you might as well start by learning the games. Now poker ain't much fun unless a feller's playing for stakes. Hop Gow, you reckon you could rustle up some matches we could use for chips? And you might trot out that lice—I mean rice—wine while you're at it. This may take a little time, the kid, here, being new to the game."

Wong Duck bowed again, displaying a courtly appreciation that would have pleased his hallowed ancestors. "Me velly pleased you wastee time showing worthless person how to play 'Melican game."

For a moment conscience smote Stumpy Grampis a mighty blow, but he recovered under it. After all, somebody was bound, sooner or later, to teach this young heathen that a man learned to play poker at a price. It would be plumb foolish to pass up a chance to enlarge that fund that he, Stumpy, had been so carefully building. Maybe he'd be able to celebrate his birthday and afterwards ride back to Dryfooting on the plush cushions of a day coach—and all this in the interests of educating the alien.

"Pass me those cards," Stumpy chortled. "Fust, I'll show you how we shuffle 'em. Son, we're gonna spend a mighty pleasant time together. Mighty pleasant!"

17

Yes, Stumpy would have made a mighty fine addition to the one-man posse which was storming Jake Kelhorn's hideout, and Rowdy, herding the Rimrock Kid's freed broomtails down into the canyon's narrow opening, smiled joyously with the thought. Stumpy could contribute a few wild *yippee-e-e-s* and a salvo of gunshots, but Rowdy was doing a fair job on his lonesome. Noise was the nucleus of this attempted deception. Thundering hoofs, wild shouts, and the banging of Rowdy's six-shooter mingled in a cacophony that would have given a Comanche a splitting headache.

There would likely be guards posted at either end of this canyon, and the thought gave Rowdy momentary pause and sent his eyes sweeping the towering walls. Nothing stirred, not even a mouse. Kelhorn had felt so sure that no one would stumble upon this place that he hadn't even bothered to set men to watching the openings. Not today, anyway. Then Rowdy was struck with another thought. Supposing Kelhorn and his crew had left the canyon while Rowdy and his friends had been busying themselves elsewhere? A fine climax to endeavor it would be to come hooting and hollering into the canyon to find it empty!

But no, Rowdy and his wild, long-maned assistants were now down into the canyon which had broadened out considerably, and, through the thick cloud of dust sired by several dozen unshod hoofs, Rowdy could make out frantic movement ahead. A few guns were barking, and Rowdy felt lead tug at his sombrero brim, but most of the hideout's occupants were in wild retreat, running for their saddled horses and vaulting to their backs, hauling those horses around and aiming them toward the far end of the canyon. The ruse was working! Jake Kelhorn's crew was convinced that something approximating a troop of cavalry was descending upon them.

But not Kelhorn himself. The boldest of them all, and the shrewdest, Kelhorn had apparently noticed that while a great many horses were approaching there was a scarcity of riders among them. Kelhorn was bawling at his retreating men and gesticulating with one arm; the other arm was employed with tugging at Nan and attempting to drag her through the doorway of that lean-to shack. Nan was giving him a fight, just as Rowdy had suspected she would, but her strength was puny compared to Kelhorn's.

There was nothing for Rowdy to do but go forward. He couldn't have stopped the mad stampede of the Kid's oreanas if he'd wanted. Those broomtails were out to make a record at running, and Rowdy's mount, catching the spirit of the affair, was determined not to be outdone. The reputation of civilized horses versus primitive ones was clearly at stake, and Rowdy's saddler was obviously of a mind to defend his cultural superiority to the last gasp. Thus it was from a pitching saddle that Rowdy aimed carefully at Kelhorn, placing the shot high, for Rowdy was mindful that Nan might be endangered when the cap was cracked. The gun bucked back against Rowdy's palm, and Kelhorn's sombrero lifted and went sailing.

Rowdy, himself, was properly astonished at his marksmanship under the circumstances, but Kelhorn was even more impressed. With a howl of rage and fear, Winged-H's foreman released Nan and went scurrying to his own horse which was tied to a corral and was rearing frantically, terror-possessed as that band of wild horses swept ever nearer. Kelhorn got into the saddle and jerked at the tie-rope and went clattering after his departing

men. And, with the enemy in complete rout, Rowdy
roared onward.

Nan, he saw, was astute enough to be keeping to the
doorway of the shack. The canyon here was so broad that
Rowdy's little band of broomtails was not likely to trample
everything and anything, but those horses were running
now with blind fear as a lash. Rowdy thundered past the
girl, seeing her face light with both recognition and astonishment, and he howled, "Go back!" and pointed behind
him. "The Kid's waiting!"

Then Rowdy was past her and following the wild horse
band to the far end of the canyon which funneled down
into another narrow slot. The wild horses, bunching together, were streaming into that slot, but here Rowdy
hauled hard on his reins, almost somersaulting his mount
over backwards, and he got out of the saddle and darted
into a scattering of shoulder-high boulders. He glanced
behind him, trying to peer through the thick dust haze for
a glimpse of the shack and the girl, but a slight turn of the
canyon obstructed his view. But Nan was safe enough
now; the Kid would see to that.

The Kid, though, was likely to need his back protected.
Rowdy knew that the game was far from won as yet.
Kelhorn had been convinced that his crew had been
duped, and Kelhorn was somewhere beyond this canyon,
overtaking his men and talking them out of their blind
panic. With the wild horse band doubtless now scattered
through the canyon maze, Kelhorn would be turning back
this way, and Rowdy, therefore, was posting himself here
to give him a warm welcome when he did. One man could
keep a hundred from coming through yonder narrow slot,
and meanwhile the Kid would be carrying Nan to safety.

Rowdy could depend on the Kid. That wild horse
hunter might have to fight against an urge to come on
through the canyon in search of Rowdy, but the Kid had

his orders and the Kid had agreed to obey them. The Kid's job was to get Nan safely to his camp, and Nan's very presence would restrain the Kid from any foolish heroics such as keeping to Rowdy's trail. Rowdy smiled a satisfied smile and rolled himself a cigarette. The plan was pat. He almost wished that Kelhorn would hurry back. The abrupt ending of all this excitement had left Rowdy with an unsated feeling.

It was a half hour before hoofs clopped against the rocky trail, and then horsemen appeared in the narrow slot that was the backdoor to this canyon. Jake Kelhorn was at the head of them, but the fact that Kelhorn was well aware that things might not be as they seemed was evidenced by the wary way in which he rode. His dark and sinister face was alert, and Rowdy grinned widely as he leveled his six-shooter atop the boulder that sheltered him, sighted carefully, and triggered. Kelhorn swerved sideways in his saddle as a bullet buzzed past his ear; the canyon walls echoed the shot, and then Kelhorn was wheeling his horse and his men were aping his action, and the group disappeared in sudden retreat.

But they didn't go far. From around a turn, Kelhorn's voice rose, the echoes multiplying it. "Dow?" he called experimentally. "Rowdy Dow?"

"Make your speech," Rowdy invited.

"I'm tired of stumbling over you every time I turn around," Kelhorn shouted, and then, from the sound of things, jogged his horse closer. "You're on the wrong side of the fence, Dow. I know what Hackett's offered you. He told me what he had in mind when he wrote that letter to you. Ten percent of Griffen's Gold. Throw in with us, Dow, and help us lay our hands on that saddle and we'll cut you in on an equal share when we divvy up."

The longer Kelhorn was here, Rowdy remembered, the more time the Kid would be having to get safely back to

camp. "What makes you think that Faust's saddle has the
secret of Griffen's Gold?" Rowdy asked. "Maybe it isn't
the saddle Tolbert meant when he wrote his poem."

"It has to be. You see, I know that Hackett's daughter
ran off with a fellow named Faust years ago. Likewise I
know that Tolbert liked Esmerelda a lot. That's been
bunkhouse talk at the Winged-H for a long time. It
wouldn't fit that Faust, who must be young Nat Faust's
dad, would show up with a kak called the Devil's Saddle
not long after Tolbert had sent Hackett the poem. Not
unless it was the saddle that Tolbert meant."

So Kelhorn had known about Esmerelda and young Nat
Faust! Yet that was not so surprising, and it also explained
why Kelhorn, from the first, had felt that Faust's saddle
was worth possessing at any cost.

"No deal," Rowdy said emphatically. "I got to look at
myself in the glass every morning when I shave. I'll make
a prettier sight if I string along with the other gang."

Some sort of whispered consultation was held beyond
the turn. Then Kelhorn's voice exploded profanely. "We'll
gun you out of there, Dow," he threatened. "You can't
hold us back forever!"

"Want to bet?" Rowdy demanded.

He expected a salvo of shots, and they came obligingly
enough. He couldn't glimpse any men; they'd apparently
gotten down from their horses and taken to the shelter of
rocks, but there was a wide clearance between the boulders where Rowdy hunkered and the opening into the
slot. Rowdy returned the fire just to keep things interest-
ing, carefully reloaded his six-shooter and waited. There
was an hour of this, and another; the sun tipped low in the
west and dropped beyond the canyon's rim, and the darkness began gathering. Rowdy was thirsty and hungry and
altogether bored, and he wondered what the night would
bring. They might try rushing him.

Once Rowdy was almost certain that he heard the ring of shod hoofs upon rock, but he couldn't be sure. Guns were barking at the time. Kelhorn, that past master of canyon strategy, might be splitting his force again, maneuvering some of his men around so that they could enter the canyon from its other end and thus pocket Rowdy. But it didn't seem likely that Rowdy could be so important at this stage of the game. Rowdy, at the moment, represented a barrier to the most direct way of taking the trail of Nan. The girl would be Kelhorn's real goal—the girl and the saddle which might be his if he held Nan hostage. Come to think of it, there hadn't been any firing for several minutes. Perhaps Kelhorn had given up the notion of going through this canyon and was already heading elsewhere, hoping that luck might favor him in an attempt to overtake the girl before she got out of the badlands.

But Rowdy couldn't be sure, and the only thing to do was to hold his post regardless. By grab, he was much like that Dutch younker who'd poked his fist into a hole in a dike and thereby saved his country. But Rowdy was far too practical to enjoy being a hero when the chore held as much discomfort as this one did. It turned cold with darkness, and the night was a sullen one with a hint of rain in the air. It was one of the longest nights in Rowdy's life. An hour after darkness he'd decided that Kelhorn had indeed gone elsewhere, but Rowdy chose to stay. Stumbling around in these canyons in this pitch might be a good way of breaking his neck.

No, there was nothing to do but bide his time until morning, and this he did, dozing intermittently. Twice he was awakened by some sound of the night and was certain that someone was creeping upon him. He fired in the general direction of the sound both times, and the second time a rodent squealed in pain. Rowdy groaned, cursed the badlands, and dozed off again.

But the sound that awakened him near dawn was most definitely the scrape of a bootsole on rock.

Rowdy jerked to full consciousness, felt cautiously along his cartridge belt and reloaded his gun. The first light, gray and deceptive, was lifting the pall of night from the canyon, and Rowdy, listening intently, heard the boot-sole scrape again. Over yonder, where the boulders were thick. He fired a high, experimental shot, heard a muted curse; and a man scurried to the protection of a big rock. A moment later Rowdy was ducking for better cover too; a bullet chipped rock near his head, the lead ricocheting mournfully. So Kelhorn's men were still hereabouts!

One of them at least. One who'd probably been left behind to insure Rowdy's staying here while the others took Nan's trail. And this one, under cover of darkness, had managed to maneuver this close! Rowdy glimpsed the tip of a sombrero showing above yonder rock, and he exposed himself momentarily, took a snap-shot at the Stetson and then dodged back. Lead barked angrily in reprisal; Rowdy counted to ten slowly, under his breath, and then inched himself around the rock until his eyes were exposed. He bobbed quickly back as he saw a hand with a gun poking into view. The bullet drove a rocky splinter past Rowdy's nose.

Here was a deadlock which, Rowdy decided, was getting most annoying. If he could plant one clear shot at yonder elusive fellow it might make all the difference, and exasperation was prodding him to gamble on a try. He tossed his sombrero beyond the rock; the other's gun banged frantically and three holes appeared in the Stetson beside the one that Nan's rifle had once made. These badlands were sure hell on hats! But his hidden opponent must be exposing himself to do such expert aiming.

Sprinting around the other side of the rock, Rowdy came charging, determined to end this thing. Then he was rocking back on his heels, astonishment hauling his jaw down.

"*Stumpy!*" he cried.

"So it's you," Stumpy said sourly, rearing up from behind the rock that had sheltered him.

"Why didn't you sing out, you crazy galoot?"

"Why didn't you?" Stumpy countered. "You shot fust, and I figgered you must be one of the flour sack boys who'd sighted me."

"When did you get back?"

"Around midnight. On the freight. Wasn't a soul in Dryfooting of our acquaintance, so far as I could find out, except Catastrophe Kate, and I avoided her. Reckon I'm plumb unpopular with her after not showing up at that hearing yesterday morning. If folks wasn't in town, it followed they must be out in the badlands. I got my hoss and lit out. Got lost in these dang rocks, first thing I knew. I heard shots thisaway last night and kept moving in the direction of the sound. I reckon it must have been you shooting."

"At shadows," Rowdy confessed. "But I'm glad those shots fetched you. Get that journal?"

"Here it is," said Stumpy, drawing the object from his shirt-front. "Where's everybody?"

But Rowdy didn't answer. He'd taken the journal and was already thumbing through its time-yellowed pages. It wasn't much of an object, that journal; the fire that had demolished a wagon train had burned the back cover from it and scorched most of the pages, and it had an incompleteness to it that had made it worthless to the many men who'd long ago scanned it hoping to find a clue to Griffen's Gold. But Rowdy read avidly, turning page after page, and the light was strong in the canyon when he finally tucked the document inside his own shirt.

Stumpy said, "Wa-al, are we gonna stand here till we grow roots? Me, I could do with some breakfast."

"Eh—?" said Rowdy and recalled himself to the present. He smiled an exultant smile. A hunch had paid off and a last piece had fallen into place in a puzzle. "My horse is hereabouts someplace," he said. "Unless it strayed off in the night."

"Tied my own nag up," Stumpy said. "You should have done likewise. Rowdy, it's shore a good thing I'm back to take care of you."

They found Rowdy's mount grazing listlessly in the scrub grass that patched this rocky country, found the mount before they'd gotten out of the canyon, and Stumpy, securing his own horse, hauled himself into the saddle. "Whereaway now?" he asked.

"To the Rimrock Kid's camp," Rowdy said, and as they jogged along he explained events since Stumpy's departure for Helena. They came out of the canyons with nobody challenging them, and they rode toward that high sentinel rock with Rowdy leading the way. Stumpy said conversationally, "Hop Gow sends his regards."

"You saw him in Helena?"

"I did," Stumpy confessed morosely. "Him and a young man named Wong Duck. One of them that Hop Gow had just smuggled in from Canady. I tried to teach that young heathen how to play poker, Rowdy. You'd be plumb astonished how much beginner's luck that lad had. Trimmed me down to my toenails."

Rowdy grinned. "Wong Duck," he said, "is Hop Gow's nephew. He was born in this country. The men who have taught Wong Duck how to play poker would stretch from here to Mexico if they were laid end to end. Him and Hop Gow have been working that swindle in cahoots for years."

Whereupon Stumpy indulged himself in a litany of profanity that would have made a mule's ears drop off. It took in not only Hop Gow and Wong Duck, but all of their collective ancestors back to Confucius. Rowdy put a period to the tirade by suddenly holding up his hand for silence. "Listen!" he barked. "Hear that, Stumpy? Gunfire. Over yonder, on the other side of the big rock."

"Shore enough," said Stumpy.

"Kelhorn!" Rowdy judged. "That's why he didn't waste any more time on me yesterday. He got out of the canyons and cut sign on the Kid and Nan. Look! See that smoke spurting atop the rock? He's got our friends trapped up there, and he's holding them."

Stumpy drew his heels forward, preparatory to feeding the spurs to his mount. "Come on!" he shouted, but Rowdy got a hard grip on his partner's arm. "What can two of us do against those odds?" Rowdy snapped. "Stumpy, you head for town as fast as you can ride. Get hold of Catastrophe Kate and tell her what's going on. Fetch her out here with the biggest posse that can be organized in a hurry. I'll do what I can here till you get back."

"Catastrophe Kate!" Stumpy moaned. "Her faith in me has gone a-winging'."

"She'll listen to you," Rowdy assured him. "She promised the Kid that she wouldn't lead a posse against Kelhorn till the Kid got Nan back. But that promise doesn't need to hold now. Get going, Stumpy. Thank heavens that woman took a shine to you. We'll need her help. This looks like the showdown."

"Okay." Stumpy said with scant enthusiasm. "I'll fetch her."

He wheeled his horse, aiming it toward the distant town. Rowdy watched him go, listened a moment to the banging of guns, smiled a smile as an idea blossomed, then rode slowly forward to where besiegers and besieged swapped frantic lead.

DEADLOCKED

The western face of the sentinel rock was as smooth as saddle leather, and only a bird could ascend the pile from that side. This Rowdy saw as he approached the landmark and scrutinized it carefully. But around the rock, where the Kid's camp sprawled, the wind had carved the sandstone so that a man might make the climb. Rowdy had judged that the rock was scalable from its eastern side the first day he'd been there, and yesterday he'd seen Caleb Hackett and Nathaniel Faust start an ascent. Now there appeared to be four figures atop the rock, and Rowdy was sure the other two were Nan and the Rimrock Kid. Whoever was opposing them with raucous rifles was stationed on the far side—the only side that had to be watched to prevent an escape. It was with no astonishment that Rowdy rounded the rock to find Kelhorn's renegade crew strewed out at a distance among littering boulders, making it hot for those who were perched aloft.

No, the astonishment was all on Kelhorn's side, for Rowdy came riding boldly into the Kid's deserted camp, his reins wrapped around his saddle horn, his hands held aloft, his knees guiding the horse. A wild shout of surprise went up from besiegers and besieged alike, the rifles fell silent, those aloft hesitating to shoot for fear of hitting Rowdy whom they'd obviously recognized, while the Winged-H crew was too paralyzed for the moment to press triggers.

But this paralysis held them no longer than it takes a watch to tick. The hardcase riders came swarming from the sheltering rocks, surrounding Rowdy and laying rough hands on him. Pablo Diablo had a knife in his fist and an avid eagerness in his dusky face, but Jake Kelhorn, no great believer in the patron saint of Guadeloupe and therefore unconvinced that Providence was playing on the square in giving such bounty into his hands, eyed Rowdy suspiciously.

"What kind of a sandy is this, Dow?" he demanded.

Rowdy's choir boy face had that look of cherubic innocence he sometimes chose to assume. "I see you haven't got the saddle," he said. "Otherwise you wouldn't be keeping that bunch penned upstairs. Did the Kid take it aloft with him?"

"What difference does that make to you?"

"I could maybe get it for you, Jake."

Kelhorn's eyes lighted, but a scowl darkened them quickly. "You trying to say you're willing to throw in with us now? To hell with you, Dow! I wouldn't trust you any further than I could toss yon big rock."

"Is that a Christian attitude to take?" Rowdy admonished him with mock severity. "No, I'm not here to throw in with you. But I know a showdown when I see one. You want the saddle. You can't get to it—not with guns upstairs—but you can keep those others from coming down and getting away. You can hold them there till they run out of bullets or grub, and you can hope that nobody shows up from town meanwhile. Catastrophe Kate, for instance. I'm here to make you a dicker, Jake. Let me go up above. I'll talk the folks into giving you the saddle. Once you get it, your end of the bargain will be to clear out and let us alone. Fair enough?"

Kelhorn's eyes narrowed. "Why should you be willing to do that?"

Rowdy shrugged. "It's the only way to break this dead-lock. You've had the saddle before and it slipped away from you. Maybe we'll get it back again. I'll take that chance."

Jake Kelhorn debated thoughtfully for a long, silent moment. Then: "There's something loco here," he growled. "But I reckon I've got nothing to lose. It won't make much difference to me whether we've got you hog-tied back yonder in the boulders or penned upstairs with the rest of them. And that's just where you'll be if you don't dump down that saddle if I let you make the climb!"

"You'll get the saddle," Rowdy promised.

He shook off such hands as were still fastened upon him, dropped to the ground, shouldered through the group and approached the eastern face of the high rock. Kelhorn's men moved quickly back toward the boulders, thus sheltering themselves from any bullets that might pepper from above now that Rowdy's presence would no longer be staying the trigger fingers of the besieged. One of the crew led Rowdy's horse into the rocks. Rowdy began to climb, and he found a series of crude steps cut into the face of the rock. This wasn't nature's capricious work, he judged; doubtless Indians had used the rock for an observation post from which to scan the country in days gone by. He toiled upward and at last stood on the top of the sentinel rock.

This summit was wide and flat except for rocky protuberances at each end. And up here were the four he'd expected to find; they came crowding to him eagerly, and Rowdy grinned. "Good morning," he said brightly. "I see you've got the saddle here, Kid. I hope you likewise had time to fetch along grub and water before Kelhorn sewed you up."

"Plenty of grub," the Kid said. "I got it from my camp. But darn little water. We'll have to go easy on it. Yep, we had a little time before Kelhorn nailed us here. That was this morning, early. Yesterday, that deal of yours worked fine at Kelhorn's hideout canyon. After you'd gone on through, I rode in and found Nan running to meet me. I stuck by your orders and fetched her here. We waited until dark for you to show up, then spent the night at my camp. This morning Hackett climbed up here to see if he could spot you. Instead, he saw Kelhorn's boys a-coming."

"I kept them busy in the canyons for a while," Rowdy said. "Just before dark they gave up the idea of smoking me out. They must have circled through the canyons during the night and picked up sign of you. Maybe they spotted Caleb up here on the rock."

"Hackett shouted a warning to us," the Kid went on. "My first idea was to get on horses and try and outrun that Winged-H bunch. I gave that up pronto. We were one horse short and Nan would have had to double up with somebody else. And there wasn't time to get to any of my wild ones that might be gentle enough to ride. I snatched up the Devil's Saddle, some grub, water, and ammunition, and we all climbed up here."

Rowdy, spying the grub sack, was delving into it. "You did the right thing," he judged.

A grim intensity harshened the Kid's face. "We could hear what you just told Kelhorn. Yesterday you said it went against your grain to think of giving him the saddle. Now you aim to do it. Why, Rowdy? We can hold out up here for a long time."

"Yesterday was yesterday," Rowdy mumbled, his mouth full of food. "Stumpy's back, amigo. I've sent him to Dryfooting for Catastrophe Kate. My idea is to stall Kelhorn along until a posse gets here. Meanwhile, I figured I might just as well be up here with the rest of you, so I schemed a way to get Kelhorn to let me make the climb."

Far below, Kelhorn's voice rose angrily. "Dow, where's that saddle? Toss it down, you double-dealing polecat!"

The Kid said, "The four of us did a lot of talking last night. Hackett here told us all about Tennyson Tolbert and the poem and Griffen's Gold. That poem starts off with some palaver about a Devil's Saddle. Now I know why Kelhorn was after that kak from the first. It fits in with the poem somehow. My guess is that inside the saddle there's a map showing where Tolbert re-buried the gold. I don't like the idea of handing the saddle over to Kelhorn!"

Rowdy glanced at Caleb Hackett. That crusty old codger was standing hipshot, and beside him was Nan, her face radiant and her arm linked through his, and on her other side was Nathaniel Faust. Rowdy said, "We're turning the saddle over to Kelhorn, Kid. I promise you we won't be making a mistake."

Caleb Hackett scowled. "Let Kelhorn have it. Let him have it, blast his renegade soul! If Jake takes the saddle and clears out, we'll all get away with our hides whole. That's the important thing. I've gotten a granddaughter out of the deal. What in thunderation do I care about the gold?"

The Rimrock Kid shrugged, picked up that ancient kak from where it lay, walked toward the rim of the rock and heaved it over. "Here's the saddle!" he shouted.

They heard the kak thud far below; they saw Kelhorn's crew dare the open space as the group went running across the clearing from the shelter of far boulders and then ran back, carrying the saddle with them. The Winged-H men disappeared, but their voices could still be heard, a wild babble of talk.

Time passed—five minutes, ten, fifteen—and the five atop the rock were silent and waiting. At last Hackett cursed softly. "They're not taking the saddle and leaving," he said. "Not by a jugful."

"I didn't figure they would," Rowdy said. "Jake Kelhorn wasn't likely to keep any such bargain."

"Then, why—?" the Kid began angrily, but Rowdy held up his hand. "Listen!"

Kelhorn's voice came angrily from the rocks. "You've crooked us, Dow!" he stormed. "We've cut this saddle into a million pieces. *There's nothing inside it—nothing at all!* It's just another old kak!"

Rowdy grinned at his friends. "You see why I was willing to give it to them? It's worthless. Tennyson Tolbert had a scheme to pull your leg, Hackett. You were supposed to jump at the notion that the saddle Faust had was the one Tolbert was talking about in his poem, and you were supposed to pay Faust a high price for it. And Tolbert would have been laughing in his grave when you did what Kelhorn has just now done—pulled the saddle apart and found it worthless."

Hackett scowled. "You mean the whole thing was a hoax? That Tolbert never did find Griffen's Gold?"

"Yes, he found it," Rowdy said. "And he gave you a fair chance to lay your hands on it. But he couldn't resist dragging a red herring across your path with that old kak."

Down below the rifles began banging, and instantly the five withdrew farther from the eastern rim. They were comparatively safe up here; the height of this rock meant that Kelhorn's crew had to fire at a forty-five degree angle, and, by the simple means of keeping back from the rim, the besieged were beyond the Winged-H crew's range of vision. They, in turn, could venture to the rim and pour lead down upon those men in the rocks, but there was little profit in that. Better to conserve their lead against any attempt of the enemy to scale the rock. It was a deadlock, pure and simple.

But Stumpy would be coming with a posse.

Rowdy rinsed his mouth sparingly from the water can, glanced at the sun and saw that it was now past noon. A quick calculation of miles and minutes indicated that it would likely be mid-afternoon before Stumpy would be back with help. Rowdy weighed the notion of telling Kelhorn about the coming posse and decided it best not to. Kelhorn might light out, and Kelhorn, kept here, would mean that the man would end up in the Dryfooting calaboose once again. Today might see the finish to Kelhorn and his dream of easy dollars. Rowdy decided to encourage wrath.

"Hey, Kelhorn," he called. "You're not keeping your end of the bargain. You were supposed to light out once you got the saddle. You got it, didn't you?"

An angry oath split the air. "You bet I got it, Dow. But whatever Tolbert put into it was taken out. And whatever that was, you folks up there have got it. And I'm going to get it!"

"The map you mean?" Rowdy cried jeeringly. "The map that was hidden inside the saddle? Come on up and get it."

For reply there was an angry burst of riflefire, and then, Kelhorn's men apparently realizing the futility of such aimless tossing of lead, the guns went silent. But shortly thereafter there was another flurry of sound, the wild beat of hoofs over rocky ground. Rowdy peered from the rim, risking exposing himself to a stray shot in order to have a look, and he saw a rider rounding the rock and streaking westward—a diminutive rider perched upon a fast horse. Pablo Diablo.

Nan was reaching for the rifle Nathaniel Faust had fetched along, but Rowdy got to the Winchester first. He crossed the rock to its western rim, a distance of about seventy-five feet, and he sighted carefully and let loose a couple of bullets, but Pablo, zig-zagging, was putting distance between himself and the rock at a rapid pace and was an elusive target as he headed in the direction of the Winged-H.

"Gone for food or more bullets, likely," Rowdy said with satisfaction. "That means they intend to stay here. Another hour or two and they'll wish they hadn't."

But his elation turned quickly to chagrin. Kelhorn's voice reached them again from those distant rocks. "How's the shooting up there?" Kelhorn demanded. "Mighty poor, I reckon. I can still hear the hoof beats of Pablo's horse. He's gone to the ranch, Dow. For some dynamite we keep there for a reservoir we've been planning to build. When he brings that dynamite back, we aim to blast that rock out from under you!"

Rowdy bethought himself of the mythical map about which he'd been taunting Kelhorn. "You'll lose your last chance at Griffen's Gold if we go chasing the birds!" he shouted.

"I've seen through your game, Dow," Kelhorn retorted. "You figger that Catastrophe Kate's out looking for me. On account of that jailbreak the other night. You figger that sooner or later her posse will show up. Likely you're right. But when that dynamite gets here, you're gonna get a choice. Either you'll lead me to Griffen's Gold, or you'll hear the biggest bang you ever heard!"

Now that, Rowdy decided, went to show what sort of pitfall a man might tumble into when he got careless with the truth. Kelhorn was now convinced that the saddle had held a map and that Rowdy or his friends had it. Crossing to the western rim, Rowdy looked down upon a panorama of badlands and scanned the horizon in the direction of Dryfooting. An hour passed, and another, and still he stayed at this post, and then he made out a minute figure far to the west. That lone horseman was leading a pack animal, and the rider was taking a circuitous route and giving the sentinel rock a wide berth. Pablo Diablo.

Rowdy glanced again at the sun and made another calculation of miles and minutes. There was something wrong—almighty wrong. Pablo Diablo was returning with the dynamite; and the showdown, the real showdown, was almost at hand. Everything depended upon Stumpy Grampis now. But if Rowdy was any good at arithmetic, Stumpy should have been back here at least thirty minutes ago. And, in the direction of Dryfooting, there was no lifting dust of a rescue party to be seen.

19

TO FETCH A POSSE

Stumpy Grampis hit Dryfooting at high noon, an hour when even the more vigorous citizens were apt to have a greater interest in putting their feet under a dinner table than in thrusting those same feet into stirrups to go larruping over the landscape. Thus Stumpy, no man to miss a meal himself, was acutely aware that it wasn't the most propitious time to organize a posse. No siree. But Stumpy had had many badland miles for reflection upon certain prevailing conditions and had thereby caught the spirit of this mission upon which he'd been sent, and in him now, full flowered, was a stubborn intent that would brook no interference. By grab, Rowdy was likely up to his ears in trouble at this very moment! A posse was going to head out of this town, and shortly, even if Stumpy had to personally boot a few gents into saddles!

And so he rode the length of a somnolent street, smelling the beguiling smells that wafted from restaurants and manfully refusing to succumb to them. There'd be time for eating later. The gauntlet of temptation behind him, he stepped down from his saddle before the jail and jangled his spurs inside. Catastrophe Kate was here, her two hundred and twenty-five pounds scrooched down into the swivel chair behind her desk, a cigar slanting from her mouth. Her broad face showed scant delight as Stumpy made his entry.

"Howdy, Katharine," Stumpy said, sweeping off his sombrero and making his most flourishing bow. "Yuh're lookin' as purty as a little desert flower unfoldin' its petals in the sunshine."

"Don't give me that!" Catastrophe Kate interjected with a black and forbidding scowl. "Just where were you yesterday morning when that hearing came off?"

"Wa-al now, Katharine, that's a mighty involved story and I ain't rightly got the time to spin it now. You see, Rowdy sent me to fetch you and a posse out to the badlands. Rowdy's got Jake Kelhorn and his crew cornered, but he'll maybe need a little help fetchin' 'em in. It shore pleasures me, Katharine, to be able to help you catch that jail-bustin' son."

Catastrophe Kate's eyes gleamed with a sudden interest, but suspicion renewed her scowl. "I want Kelhorn, of course," she confessed. "Did you see what that confounded Winged-H bunch did to my jail? And I know that Kelhorn must be out in the badlands. But I can't bust a promise, and I promised the Rimrock Kid that I'd stand pat till he had a chance at getting the Bolton girl away from Kelhorn."

"You don't have to pay no never mind to that promise," Stumpy hastily assured her. "Everything's changed. The Kid got the gal, all right. But Kelhorn—"

"You've talked to the Kid?"

Stumpy kneaded his sombrero in his hands and looked

at his toes for inspiration. A plague on a stubborn woman! "Wa-al, no," he admitted. "But Rowdy said—"

Catastrophe Kate came to a ponderous stand and shook a huge finger at Stumpy. "Gabriel, what am I to do with you?" she demanded. "How can I possibly believe you when you're so thoroughly under the influence of Rowdy Dow. And what reason have I got to trust him? Sure, he bagged Kelhorn at the opera house the other night, but he never would tell just what game he, himself, was playing. And whatever he's up to, I'm afraid you're just his tool. How do I know whether there's a mite of truth in anything you're saying?"

Stumpy said desperately, "Now, look! If you'll just pin yore faith in me and organize a posse—"

Catastrophe Kate snorted. "Pin my faith in *you*? Twice I trusted you, Gabriel, and twice you betrayed that trust. Next to a drinking man, I never could abide an undependable man."

Stumpy sighed a long and hopeless sigh. A varied past had given him experience in the handling of cattle, horses, mules, and oxen, but how did a man go about bending a woman to his will? Especially a woman as adamant as Catastrophe Kate McCandless? Patently she considered Stumpy Grampis as no paragon of truth, and patently arguments and persuasions were only going to waste precious time. So Stumpy again sought inspiration, and, finding it, abruptly changed his tactics.

"Reckon you're right about me being a tool of Rowdy's," he said sadly. "Never could savvy just how he keeps me under his spell, but it's shore the truth. It's like I was a bird and he was a snake, I reckon." Here Stumpy paused to sigh again. "When I met you, Katharine, I saw a means to escape from that slavery. Maybe I didn't have no right to dream of a little nest, just big enough for a couple of people the size of you and me. What is it the poet said about them sweet words, 'It might have been . . .'?"

"Gabriel," Kate said, "are you trying to tell me you might have considered marriage?"

Stumpy adopted what he hoped was a coy look. "If you can catch me, you can shore hog-tie me!" he said. And with that he turned and darted through the doorway.

Behind him he heard Catastrophe Kate lumbering around her desk, but before she could gain the doorway, Stumpy had slanted across the street to the porch of a mercantile store and was vanishing into its interior. From this sanctuary he paused, seeing the sheriff appear, look to left and right, and then head down the street. Stumpy grinned thoughtfully and had a look around the establishment in which he found himself.

He'd gotten one recruit for a posse, but even Catastrophe Kate would have to have backing when she went up against the renegade Winged-H crew. Stumpy's work was far from finished.

This store was one of those emporiums in which a man could buy anything from a shirt button to a fancy saddle. There were shelves piled high to the ceiling; there were displays of canned goods, and heaped counters, and three toiling clerks as well as the manager. A few bonneted shoppers were in the store, and one of these was being attended to by the manager, though not with any show of graciousness. Stumpy studied the manager, noting a truculent jaw and a pair of close-set eyes. Patently here was a man of short temper, a man who wished to be at his dinner and whose temper was all the shorter because hunger gnawed at him. Stumpy approached the counter, and, while the manager was wrapping his customer's purchase, Stumpy thrust his hand into an open cracker barrel.

"Take your claw out of there, stranger!" the manager

snapped. "I'm tired of having half my profits eaten up by every saddle bum who comes along!"

"Shore," Stumpy said dreamily. The customer turned away, and Stumpy added: "Me, I'd like a quart of coal oil."

"Fetch a can?"

Stumpy shook his head; the manager glared at him, muttered something uncomplimentary under his breath and vanished into a rear storeroom. He was back in a few minutes with a brimming coal oil can, a potato stuck on its spout, and the can was extended to Stumpy. That worthy took it and would have turned on his heel except that the manager said ominously, "Let's see the color of your money."

"Shucks," Stumpy said blandly, "why should I pay for this when I don't aim to take it out of the store?"

And with that he pulled the potato from the spout, up-ended the can and poured the full quart into the cracker barrel.

The roar that boiled upward out of the wide chest of the mercantile man was the same kind of sound by which a volcano announces that after a few centuries of hibernation it has decided to spew forth destruction again. Placing a palm on the counter, the manager came vaulting over the obstruction, but Stumpy kicked over the cracker barrel, full into the path of the charging man, and the fellow sprawled over this.

"Zeke—Harry—Jim!" he was bawling to his clerks. "Grab the crazy galoot! I'll take the hide off him!"

Bonneted shoppers were shrieking to high heaven. Before the astonished clerks could get into action or their employer could pick himself from the floor, Stumpy had gained the door, wrenched it open, and was gone. He went running along the porch, dropped to the ground, scurried to the rear of the store building and headed down the alley, grateful that Catastrophe Kate had not been in sight. Behind him pandemonium reigned; he heard the banging of the store door, the bull-like roar of the manager, the babble of the clerks, and Stumpy, grinning, legged along.

Four more recruits for the posse!

Stumpy ran only a short distance. Soon he found himself at the rear door of a blacksmith shop. He paused here, catching his breath and speculating upon a new possibility for deviltry. The blacksmith, that big and burly man who'd been at the opera house the other night, was engaged in shoeing a most refractory horse, and his apprentice was helping him. The two were sweating mightily; for here was a mount that should have been thrown and staked out, a rope around each foot, while the hoofs were trimmed and the shoes nailed on. But some professional pride in the blacksmith was making him do this job the hard way, the apprentice trying vainly to soothe the horse while the blacksmith toiled.

This spectacle Stumpy watched in silence, and then, without attracting attention to himself, since the pair in the shop were far too busy with the horse to notice him, he very carefully picked up a handful of small pebbles from the alley.

"Two onto one is Nigger fun!" Stumpy suddenly shouted in a shrill voice and pelted the interior of the blacksmith shop with the pebbles.

It was like stirring up a gigantic hornet's nest. The horse, stung by a sharp-edged rock, launched a kick at the leather-aproned lap of the blacksmith, a kick that almost sent the man into his own forge. At the same time the mount tried taking a bite out of the apprentice who was holding its head. As Stumpy went legging it on down the alley, he could hear the thud of hoofs against the blacksmith shop walls, the clatter of falling iron, the wild shouts of anger and dismay that came from the blacksmith and his apprentice. The outraged pair came into the alley, their fists clenched and hoisted, just as Stumpy bobbed out of view between buildings.

The posse business was certainly picking up!

Gaining the street, he abruptly turned back. Down the boardwalk the mercantile store manager was charging, his three clerks trailing him, and if ever a man had mayhem on his mind, it was that mercantile store galoot. But before Stumpy was spied, he'd dodged back into the shelter between the buildings, and he retreated to the alley again, mindful that he might be running into the arms of the angry blacksmith and his apprentice. But that pair had obviously headed for the street by way of the passage between two other buildings, for Stumpy found no one awaiting him. Legging on up the alley, he turned into the rear door of the Tarantula Saloon.

Here was familiar ground, remembered from his first night in Dryfooting, and Stumpy came through that rear room, littered with cased whiskeys and beer barrels, and by this means into the barroom. Four men were engaged in a game of poker that had risen to such a crescendo of interest that the players were unmindful that it was meal-time. Crossing the sawdust-sprinkled floor, Stumpy skirted the scattering of tables and chairs, and bellied up to the bar. The barkeep eyed him with no great interest and said, all in one breath, "What'llitbe?"

"Some hair restorer," said Stumpy.

The apron shrugged. "They call it by a lot of names," he said and reached for a whiskey bottle.

Beyond the batwings the boardwalks rumbled to many feet, and somebody was demanding in an angry voice if anybody had sighted a sawed-off little squirt with a down-tilted mustache. The bartender inclined his head and said, "Wonder what the ruckus is about?"

"Dunno," said Stumpy. "It's no time of day to be raising a hullabaloo. What's the matter with folks in this
town? Ain't they got any consideration for peace and
quiet?"

The apron extended the whiskey bottle. Stumpy eyed it
with great disdain. "Yuh heard me!" Stumpy growled. "I
said hair restorer. I bet a feller I could grow hair on a pool
ball. You got a sign out front that says you sell bottled
goods. Hair restorer comes in bottles. You tryin' to delude
the public?"

"Look," said the bartender, matching Stumpy's own
show of belligerency, "I've just remembered you. You're
one of those galoots who started a gun ruckus in here a
few nights back. A natural trouble-maker, eh? Now this is
an orderly establishment and if you think—"

Stumpy had gotten his inspiration. "No trouble," he
said mildly. "There's just one galoot I've got it in for, and
when I sight him, the fireworks start. Can't help it, but I
go completely loco when I see that sidewinder."

"And who's the gent who gets you riled up?" the apron
asked.

"*Him!*" Stumpy roared and pointed a finger at his own
reflection in the bar mirror. And with that he dragged out
his gun and snapped a shot at the mirror that brought the
glass down in a hundred showering fragments. Then
Stumpy was whirling on one heel, the other foot raised,
and he shouted, "Gambling's a device of the devil!" and
he kicked over the card table, sending chips and cards
scattering every direction.

The apron had gone bobbing under the bar. Stumpy
made it to the batwings just one jump ahead of a shower
of buckshot as the barkeep roared into view again, a shotgun in his hands. Six-shooters were sounding too as the
irate poker players got into action. But Stumpy was out-

side and pounding along the planking, putting distance between himself and the saloon.

Five new recruits!

Ahead was the store manager and his clerks; the four sighted Stumpy simultaneously, and Stumpy went veering across the street. Thus he almost ran into the arms of Catastrophe Kate who suddenly materialized in a doorway. Stumpy took a quick turn to the right, bobbed between two buildings, heard the Tarantula bartender's shotgun boom again, and then Stumpy was heading up an alley at a hard run.

He got to the jail-building without mishap; he came around a corner of that structure, hoping frantically that nobody had as yet had the presence of mind to remove his horse. But the mount was still standing, and he got into the saddle without touching the stirrups. Jerking at the tie-rope, he swung the mount, kicked it to a high gallop, and headed down the street.

Now indeed he was running a gauntlet. From everywhere people came converging to lay violent hands upon him, but he was moving too fast for them. He saw the wrath-contorted faces of the store manager, the blacksmith and his apprentice. He heard Catastrophe Kate lustily bellowing his name and ordering him to stop. He saw the Tarantula bartender waving his now empty shotgun and shaking his fist, the four poker players massed behind him, flourishing six-shooters. And then he saw all these people hurrying to horses at the nearest hitchrails.

Dryfooting's main street blurred past Stumpy and was no more. The rocky underfooting of the badlands streaked beneath him, but within a quarter of a mile he paused, drew rein, and looked back. Behind a dust cloud was already rising to the sky; out of that cloud loomed horses and riders. How many? The store manager and his three clerks, the blacksmith and his apprentice, the bartender,

Catastrophe Kate, the four poker players. That made only twelve. Others must have caught the contagion of the chase, for the pursuit had nearly doubled.

Bullets began pelting around Stumpy. Again he lifted his horse to a gallop, heading as directly as he could toward that distant sentinel rock where he'd left Rowdy. He had to keep beyond the reach of those who were chasing him, for, in their present mood, they'd probably haul him back to town and hang him from the highest ridgepole. But, on the other hand, he mustn't get too far ahead of them. After all, it behooved a man who was leading a posse to keep that posse in sight.

20

SHARP SHOOTING

There were times, Rowdy Dow decided, when a man might be too confounded clever for his own good. Perched atop the sentinel rock with Caleb Hackett, Nathaniel Faust, Nan Bolton and the Rimrock Kid crowded close to him while the five watched the oncoming Pablo Diablo, it was Rowdy's thought that he'd sewed himself into a corner from which there was no escape. With Stumpy dispatched to Dryfooting to fetch a posse, it had been Rowdy's whim to talk his way to the top of this rock. After that he'd stalled for time, keeping Kelhorn here for the inevitable pay-off that was to come when the law arrived. It had been a pat scheme, but it had had one flaw of noticeable proportions. The scheme hadn't worked. Stumpy was nowhere in sight, but Pablo was returning with dynamite that would blast them all from this rock.

That Kelhorn would carry out his threat went without saying. Kelhorn had seen through Rowdy's game of keeping the Winged-H crew waiting here, and Kelhorn was now desperate enough to resort to anything. Kelhorn meant to break this deadlock mighty fast, and Pablo was fetching the means by which Kelhorn could make the last move. Kelhorn was going to play a hole card. Unless Pablo could be stopped.

Therein lay the ghost of a chance, and Rowdy turned quickly to Nan. "You're the handiest with a rifle," he said. "Do you think you could knock that horse from under Pablo?"

Nan raised the Winchester, squinted carefully along its barrel, then lowered the gun, shaking her head. Pablo, trailing a pack animal, was not moving swiftly, for Pablo was probably all too acutely aware of the touchy nature of the cargo he was transporting. Pablo might be wont to call upon the patron saint of Guadeloupe in emergencies, but the Mexican doubtless had small desire to meet the saint face to face. Pablo was still a considerable distance away, and he was still following the circuitous route that brought him no closer to the big rock. In short, Pablo was playing safe.

But to the five watching his progress with intent interest, the diminutive Mexican gradually grew a bit larger, and again Nan raised her rifle. The .30-.30 spoke, dust spurted between Pablo's saddler and the led pack animal, and instantly Pablo showed a great deal more life than he'd been displaying. He went zig-zagging away at an angle that put greater distance between himself and the rock. Nan fired again, and the Mexican's heels beat more frantically against the horse's sides.

"You've got him worried," the Kid chuckled.

"He's losing himself in those rocks, yonder," Faust observed calmly. "He'll make it a point to keep beyond rifle range the rest of the way."

"Maybe he's just staying in hiding, hoping we'll get

tired of looking for him," Rowdy said. "Keep a sharp eye out, folks."

They watched until their eyes ached, but Pablo failed to reappear. Five minutes went by . . . ten . . . fifteen . . . Rowdy remembered Stumpy again and realized that his partner was indeed hopelessly overdue. Then, suddenly, the Rimrock Kid, muttering a curse under his breath, went running to the eastern side of the rock, his six-shooter coming into his hand and beginning a wild banging. Rowdy and the others hurried to join him, but a steady barrage of bullets from Kelhorn's men drove them back from the rim. The Kid was almost weeping with rage. "Pablo outsmarted us!" he cried. "I started figgering the lay of the country, but I remembered too late. There's a long, curving canyon over yonder to the north. Pablo dipped down into it, followed the canyon, and circled around to Kelhorn and the others. They've got the dynamite down below now!"

Rowdy swept his sombrero away, dropped to his stomach and wormed to the edge of the rock. With only his eyes showing over the rim, he could look upon the clearing directly below him, and he could see the Kid's deserted camp, and he could also see the men who were dragging a dynamite case with fuse and cap affixed into a position at the base of the big rock. Only two were busy at this chore; Kelhorn and the others, still hiding in the sheltering rocks, were waiting with ready guns for anyone to show himself atop the rock. Rowdy was sighted and bullets began to drone about him. A wild desperation making him oblivious to danger, Rowdy tried peppering shots at the two who were placing the dynamite. But when a bullet clipped a lock of his hair away, he withdrew from the rim, fumbling at his cartridge belt. A wild shout went up from below; boots pounded against rocky underfooting, and when Rowdy ventured to peer again, the two were scurrying to rejoin Kelhorn and the others.

Down below, almost directly below, a long, white fuse lay coiled across the ground, a fuse that stood out starkly white, one end reaching to the dynamite case, the other end sputtering and smoking. This Rowdy saw, and butterflies went stampeding through his stomach.

"That's a five minute fuse, Dow!" Kelhorn's voice roared jeeringly. "That gives you just five minutes to make up your mind what you want to do. If there was anything in the Devil's Saddle that pointed the way to Griffen's Gold, you'd better toss it down!"

Rowdy felt the sweat start out on himself. Kelhorn and his crew hadn't been able to do much of a job with the dynamite. They hadn't toted it under an overhang on the big rock's eastern face; they'd wanted it out in view where Rowdy and his friends could watch that burning fuse. Nor had they had the means of drilling holes in the base of the rock and tamping in the explosive. Just exactly how much damage that dynamite would do when it let go was a conjecture, but this huge sentinel rock was made of sandstone, not of granite. Any way a man looked at it, this was likely to be an unhealthy spot when that fuse burned to its finish.

But would Kelhorn let that happen? Would Kelhorn wilfully destroy whatever last chance might be remaining to find out the secret that Tennyson Tolbert might or might not have left behind him? This could be a bluff—but a very fatal bluff if it were called.

Rowdy glanced at his friends. The Kid, who'd once said, "Gawd pity the galoot who marries her!" had moved to Nan and placed his arms around her. There were no words between them, but anyone could see that here at last, with death's cold breath touching them, they were admitting a truth that had been obvious from their first meeting. Caleb Hackett was fighting down a monstrous and futile anger, his wrinkled face twitching with rage as he cursed Kelhorn under his breath. But there was no fear in the man, and it was Rowdy's thought that whatever else Hackett might have been, through a bitter lifetime, he was certainly no coward. Nathaniel Faust was the calmest of all. He stood with his shoulders squared and his spine straight, and he smiled wanly. "Looks like the finish," he said.

Rowdy was remembering the night he'd ridden wildly from Dryfooting, intent upon stopping this same Nathaniel Faust from murdering Caleb Hackett. He was remembering the sensation that had been his that night—the feeling that all of them were puppets, dancing to the manipulations of the dead hand of Tennyson Tolbert. Now he had that sensation again, but with it was a satisfied feeling, the feeling that Tennyson Tolbert had somehow wrought a miracle. This was what Esmerelda Hackett would have liked to see—her father and her daughter and the man who was Nat Faust's father all standing shoulder to shoulder in the face of danger. And, seeing this, Rowdy knew that the gold didn't count with any of them. Not any more. They'd found a greater treasure.

Sighing, Rowdy thought of the ten percent that was to have been his. Then he cased his revolver and stepped boldly to the rim, outlining himself and holding his hands high. "Come on out, Kelhorn!" he shouted. "There'll be no shooting while you jerk that fuse. And once you've jerked it, I'll lead you straight to Griffen's Gold."

Jake Kelhorn reared upward among the sheltering rocks. Even at this distance Rowdy could see that the man's grin was triumphant. "Thought you'd get sensible before it was too late," Kelhorn yelled.

He took a step forward, and there was silence then, a silence in which his crew waited breathlessly, realizing that at long last they'd won; and those on the rock waited just as breathlessly, wondering if they were indeed to be reprieved. But out of that silence a thunder suddenly grew, a distant, sullen thunder, the beat of many hoofs against a trail, and intermingled with that sound was the wild shouting of many men. The Kid went darting to the western edge of the rock and turned, glancing back at the others. "Riders!" he shouted. "A sizable bunch. Heading this way from the direction of Dryfooting!"

Kelhorn had heard that sound too—and interpreted it for what it was. His grin faded and was replaced by a look of wild and desperate anger. "A posse!" he shouted. "You almost stalled long enough, eh, Dow!"

Then the man was heading back into the rocks from which he'd emerged, bellowing frantic orders to his crew as he went. An instant later the sound of hoofs against rock was ringing out, but this sound was much closer than that made by the posse. It was a sound sired by the Winged-H crew as they got up into saddles and lined out in desperate retreat, heading into the canyon where the Rimrock Kid had kept his wild horses corraled. Rowdy shouted, *"The fuse! Kelhorn, the fuse!"* But Jake Kelhorn was either too concerned with making himself scarce before the posse arrived, or else Kelhorn, in a perverse fury, was leaving them to their fate, a last, murderous act which, although it couldn't salvage victory out of defeat for the man, would at least mean the end of those who'd thwarted him.

Now there was no man to stop the five atop the rock from clambering downward, but Rowdy, peering from the height, was weak with the realization that there wasn't time to get from the rock and stop the explosion. That fuse was less than a foot long. Nor would the Dryfooting posse cover the distance before the fire reached the dynamite. Thus, at the bitter end, it looked as though Kelhorn was going to accomplish half a purpose, for who could snatch that fuse in time?

The Rimrock Kid was already running to those cut-in steps, beginning a descent, but Rowdy shouted, "Stop!" fearful that the Kid would take a tumble in his desperate haste. "Your rifle!" Rowdy shouted at Nan. "You've got to do your sharpest shooting now. It's our only chance! Can you cut that fuse with a rifle bullet? From here?"

Nan saw what he meant. Instantly she was down upon her stomach and peering over the rim. She got the rifle's stock against her cheek and took careful aim; and Rowdy stopped breathing. It was all of fifty yards from the top of this rock to the ground below, and the shot was almost straight down, a difficult one to make. And the target was that white fuse, no wider than a lead pencil and so short now as to indicate that less than a minute remained before the dynamite exploded. Nan seemed to be taking an inordinately long time aiming, and suddenly Rowdy saw to his horror that her shoulders were shaking.

"Steady!" he cried.

"Buck fever," she said jerkily. "For the first time in my life, I've got buck fever!"

Rowdy understood. On a stage she'd showed a superlative prowess with any sort of gun. Now, with the lives of all of them depending upon her shooting ability, the necessity of making a perfect shot had put too much of a strain on her nerves. Instantly Rowdy was down beside her. He got the rifle from her trembling hands, and he cradled the stock against his own cheek. He was a fair hand with a Winchester, but he'd never been called upon to do this kind of shooting before.

The fuse, so far below, seemed to waiver; he blinked his eyes and gently pressed trigger. Dirt spurted to the right of the fuse, a good three inches off target. Again he fired, coming closer to the mark this time. He was all ice and granite now, pushing the desperate need from his mind and thinking of nothing but profiting by his errors in calculation. He fired again; the fuse parted, and there wasn't the strength in him then to hold the rifle. He let it drop, and it went clattering, striking the face of the rock and caroming outward. Hauling himself back from the rim, Rowdy came to a wobbly stand, feeling very much as though it would be an easy thing to fall flat on his face just then.

They began the descent a moment later, coming down in easy stages and helping each other over the more dangerous spots. When they'd reached the ground, Rowdy strode at once to the dynamite and jerked the dead stub of the fuse from the box. It was then that a whirlwind of riders came roaring around the rock, Stumpy Grampis in the lead and Catastrophe Kate right behind him, and many others strewed out in the boiling dust. Rowdy pointed toward the canyons. "Kelhorn!" he shouted. "Over there. He just tried to blast us off the rock with this dynamite."

"Yuh see!" Stumpy shrilled. "I was telling you straight when I said a posse was needed out here!"

"You're all deputized!" Catastrophe Kate shouted at the milling riders who seemed to be concerned with surrounding Stumpy. "Get after 'em, boys. We're rounding up that bunch of skunks for keeps!"

She dominated them as a strong wind dominates a pile of tumbleweeds, scattering them before her into the canyons. They went roaring away, all but Stumpy who slipped from his jaded horse and came to Rowdy who'd seated himself on the dynamite case. Stumpy said, "Sorry I was so late. I had to raise considerable ruckus in Dryfooting to get me a posse. In fact, them boys didn't foller me out here—they chased me. We workin' on an expense account, Rowdy? It's gonna take a couple hundred dollars to square me in that there town."

"Don't worry about it," Rowdy said. "Listen to that hullabaloo over in the canyons. Kate's loaded for bear today."

"And Kelhorn won't get far," the Rimrock Kid said with a grin. "I've got half of those canyons blocked off; I use 'em for wild horse traps. Kelhorn's either going to get caught losing time trying to tear his way out of a blocked canyon, or else he's going to turn back and run straight into the arms of that posse."

"It looks," said Rowdy, "like the chores are about done."

"And you did the last one," said Nathaniel Faust. "That was mighty sharp shooting you did with that rifle."

Rowdy tried appearing properly modest, but it was obvious that masculinity which had once taken a beating from Catastrophe Kate now stood reasserted. "Nan could have done better ordinarily," he said. "She wouldn't have wasted two shots. She'd just been through too much lately."

"One thing," said Faust. "At the finish, once the fuse was lighted, you told Kelhorn you'd take him to Griffen's Gold. You were bluffing, of course, saying anything in order to get him to jerk that fuse."

Rowdy grinned. "You think so? Then just wait until six o'clock and I'll show you different. You're standing within a hoot and a holler of Griffen's Gold right now. And I'm the gent who can point out where Tennyson Tolbert buried it."

21

Shovels were fetched from the Winged-H, and it was Caleb Hackett himself who went after them. He also brought along Tennyson Tolbert's letter at Rowdy's request, and by the time the oldster had returned, quite an assorted group was waiting in the shadow of the sentinel rock. For Catastrophe Kate McCandless and her posse had come riding back out of the canyons, and with them were prisoners, the whole renegade Winged-H crew.

Said Catastrophe Kate: "I'm taking them to the big jail in Miles City. Found those flour sack hoods stuffed into their saddle-bags, and there's enough against them, including an attempt at mass murder, to put the whole kit and caboodle in stony lonesome so long they'll be tripping over their beards. These badlands will be a plumb law-abiding place from here on out."

Jake Kelhorn stood with his hands lashed behind him and his huge shoulders slumped in resignation. Thus had his dream ended, and thus was Rowdy to remember him, a man of savagery and shrewdness defeated at last.

Stumpy Grampis said, "Just remember, Katharine, that it was me and Rowdy who really tangled these galoots' twine for them. If you'll stick around, you'll find what Rowdy's game was in these badlands, and how he played it out. I ain't rightly sure myself."

A good many of the posse members were still glaring angrily at Stumpy, and that little man was making a great point of sticking very close to either Rowdy or Catastrophe Kate. But before Caleb Hackett returned there was time for much talking, and by then a new interest had gripped the posse, for where was a Dryfooting man who'd never heard of Griffen's Gold and dreamed about the finding of it? When Hackett rode up and delivered the shovels, a hushed expectancy held the crowd. Rowdy, a man to realize the dramatics of the moment, was not above playing them for all they were worth.

"Anybody got the time?" he asked.

Five people promptly informed him that it was almost six o'clock.

Tolbert's letter in his hand, Rowdy paced carefully, seemingly making some sort of mysterious calculation, and Professor Marvelo would have had a right to feel a twinge of professional jealousy just watching Rowdy perform. Apparently Rowdy was consulting the heavens, the letter, and also his own feet. His lips moved silently, but he didn't look like a man who was praying. Suddenly he pointed to a spot on the ground. "Dig here," he announced.

Ready hands reached for shovels. There were men present who weren't going to share in whatever was found, but here was the makings of a tale to be told to round-eyed grandchildren as yet unborn, and many were anxious to glean a bit of glory. Dirt and rock flew; a hole grew deeper and wider, and Rowdy, seated upon the dynamite case again, might have appeared a bit worried if anybody had looked at him close enough. But all eyes were glued upon that excavation, and suddenly a shout went up from a shovel wielder, and the diggers were down upon their hands and knees, clawing avidly. Rotting buckskin pokes came into view, a half-dozen of them, and thus, after the years, did men look upon Joshua Griffen's legendary gold.

Yet the one man who might have been displaying a wild eagerness stood quietly aside. He was Caleb Hackett, and he only said, "I'd like to know how you did it, Dow?"

"You handed me a puzzle," Rowdy said. "But only part

of the pieces were there. I've picked up a missing piece from time to time, and the job was to put them together. Once the pattern began shaping up, it was pretty plain. You might say the thing began with your girl, Esmerelda. She's the one who talked you into grubstaking Tennyson Tolbert. Later you drove Esmerelda out of your life for marrying Nat Faust. But Tolbert kept track of Esmerelda, and he knew about Nan being born, and Esmerelda and Nat Faust dying, and Nathaniel Faust, Sr. raising the girl."

Hackett nodded. "That was all made plain enough the other night when Faust, here, come to the ranch-house to kill me."

"That wasn't part of Tolbert's plan," Rowdy said. "Tolbert was a grim humorist in his way, but all the sign says he was also a square-shooter. Once I wondered why he didn't give the location of the hidden gold to Nan and forget all about you. But Tolbert was remembering that you'd grubstaked him, and, regardless of personal feelings, he was honest enough to want to square that debt before he died. Yet he wanted to make you sweat for the gold, just as he'd sweated. And I'm guessing that he had a more important scheme in his head. He wanted to bring you and your granddaughter together. So he made two moves. He shipped a saddle to Nathaniel Faust, and he sent you a riddle."

"I know it by heart," Hackett said and began intoning:

"If the Devil's Saddle's too hot for your pants
    When the April sun is hell,
Injun down from that kak and bend your old back,
    When you hear your own supper bell;
Just keep to the shade that the saddlehorn's made,
    And don't be afraid to sweat;
There's no easy way to get rich in a day,
    And you'll earn all the gold that you'll get!"

"That's it," said Rowdy. "He was telling you where he'd hidden the gold. And to start, you had to locate the Devil's Saddle. Jake Kelhorn was off chasing what he thought was the saddle and keeping you a prisoner in your own ranch house so you wouldn't get wise to him, but Kelhorn tore that saddle apart today and found it was just a plain, ordinary kak. No, the real saddle had to be something else. But how was a man to find out? Griffen's journal came to my mind; it stood to reason that if anything was in writing concerning Griffen's Gold, it must be in the journal. Yet that charred old book had been in Dryfooting for years, and nobody had got rich from it. Just the same, I sent Stumpy after the journal. Meantime I'd got into the habit of trying to find familiar shapes in the queer look of the badland rocks, just to amuse myself. The night that I rode out from town to keep you from being salivated by Faust, I saw this big rock from a distance and from an angle that made it plain to me that it was shaped something like a saddle. But I was too busy that night to think much about it. Later, Stumpy fetched me Griffen's journal."

He dug into his shirt front and produced that scorched document. "Listen to this—" he said and flipped the pages and began reading a passage. " 'We are camped tonight in the shadow of a huge rock which one of our party has observed looks not unlike a saddle. Satan's Saddle, I shall call it, for it strikes me that it should make a fine vantage point for those red imps who have been stalking us to watch our movements for many a mile . . . ' "

He glanced at his intent audience. "You see," he said, "this rock is the Devil's Saddle that Tolbert meant. Many men probably read this passage in days gone by, when the journal was on display in the Dryfooting newspaper office. Any of those men, if they'd seen the poem Tolbert sent you, Hackett, might have realized that the Devil's

Saddle was this very rock. But nobody cared about the
journal since the part that told where Griffen had originally buried his gold was destroyed. Yet you were groping
toward the truth, Hackett, when you had the notion of
looking at the journal yourself."

"Confound the riddle-spieling old fool," Hackett said
with a show of his former fire. "I was remembering that
Tolbert used to thumb through the journal whenever he
was in town. Had a notion it might lead him to the gold."

"How Tolbert found Griffen's original treasure cache,
we'll never know," Rowdy said. "He probably just stumbled upon it after many years of looking. Our worry was
where he'd buried the gold after finding it. Now we know
he buried it here and had told you so in his rime."

Hackett said, "It's beginning to make sense, but how
did you work out the rest of it?"

"By thinking," Rowdy said with a flourish. " 'If the
Devil's Saddle's too hot for your pants when the April sun
is hell, Injun down from that kak . . .' What could
Tolbert have meant by that? Now this rock runs from the
north to the south. A white man climbs off his horse from
the left side, but a redskin mounts and dismounts from
the right. It follows that once you get the idea that here is
the saddle, your next job is to climb off the saddle the way
an Injun would—on the right side. That means this side—
the east side."

Hackett's eyes widened. "I see that part of it. 'Injun
down from that kak and bend your old back, when you
hear your own supper bell . . .' "

"That made another piece that just fit into my hand,"
Rowdy admitted. "I figured that supper bell business had
to refer to the brass bell you've got out in your yard. The
Rimrock Kid told me that you used to run your ranch by
the clock and that the supper bell rang right on the dot of

six. Tolbert knew that too, of course. But what comes next? 'Just keep to the shade that the saddlehorn's made, and don't be afraid to sweat . . .' You see the idea now? That bump of a rock at the north end of the top of this rock makes the saddlehorn, and its shadow falls differently at different times of the day and of the year. But you were supposed to keep to the shade—in other words, to watch the shadow."

"I see it now," Nathaniel Faust, a silent listener, spoke up. "Tolbert buried his gold at the exact spot where the saddlehorn's shadow fell at a certain time of day and a certain season of the year. That's why his rime said, 'If the Devil's Saddle's too hot for your pants, when the *April* sun is hell . . .' He made it a point to send his letter this spring, at the same season when he'd originally reburied the gold."

"Right as rain," Rowdy agreed. " 'And don't be afraid to sweat . . .' That meant you had to dig for it. Yes, it was all in his rime. The one thing that tangled everybody was Faust's saddle. Tolbert was having his own kind of fun with that idea. You, Hackett, were supposed to jump at the notion that Faust's saddle was the one mentioned in the poem, and it followed that you'd be willing to buy that saddle at any price from Faust. But I'll always think that Tolbert had a better idea in the back of his head. This was his scheme to bring all of you together."

"And it worked," Caleb Hackett said solemnly. "If Nan will give me the chance, I want to make up for a lot of years we lost."

Jake Kelhorn, standing spread-legged, his arms lashed behind him, suddenly lunged at Rowdy, a wild fury in the man's swarthy face, but alert posse members instantly swarmed over Kelhorn, bearing him to the ground. "I just wish that dynamite had gone off!" Kelhorn roared.

"Maybe I'd never have found the gold, but none of you would have lived to enjoy it! To blazes with all of you!"

"Shut up!" Stumpy said sternly. "Want me to bend my gun-barrel between your horns?" Then, struck by a sudden thought, his voice rose shrilly. "I'm just remembering," he cried. "All that talk about a dinner bell! I ain't et today. Let's head for that ranch of yours, Hackett. Me, I'm pinin' to shove my feet under a table!"

Night had come to the badlands, a soft and luminous night blessed by a rising moon. The great ranch house of the Winged-H was aglow with lamplight and alive with merriment, even though Catastrophe Kate had long since departed for Dryfooting, taking her posse and her prisoners with her. Also, she'd taken Griffen's journal which Rowdy had asked her to return to the State Historical Library with a note of explanation and apology. Hackett and Faust and Nan and the Kid were still in the house, but Rowdy had slipped to the corral and was saddling, and Stumpy, obeying a beckoning nod of Rowdy's, had followed after him.

"I've never liked good-byes," Rowdy said. "The simplest way is just to saddle up and hit the trail. I've got to take this horse to the Dryfooting livery and swap it for my own. Anything else that has to be settled, these folks will settle among themselves. If you hadn't been so busy stuffing your face, you'd have heard the talk. Faust's trouping days are over; Hackett's invited him to make his home at the Winged-H. And now that the spread hasn't any crew, the Kid will be collecting a new one, with himself as foreman."

"After the wedding," Stumpy said. "Nan told me in private that she figgers on marrying the Kid real quick before he wakes up to the fact that he'll now be marrying money and gets some high-principled notions."

Rowdy sighed, perhaps with regret. "Cupid used a Gatling gun," he murmured, and then his face brightened. "Ten percent of Griffen's Gold will add up to around ten thousand dollars, the way Hackett figures it. He's promised to turn that dust into cash and put our share to our credit in a Miles City bank so we can have it when we want it. That will make a nice stake for us, Stumpy. If we ever get tired of being fiddle-footed, we can buy us a ranch."

He got the cinch tightened and had his hand to the saddlehorn before he realized that Stumpy had made no move to get gear onto his own horse. "You coming?" Rowdy asked.

"Wa-al, now, Rowdy, I just bin thinkin'," Stumpy said. "I sorta made a bargain with Katharine today. The deal was that if she'd catch me, I'd marry up with her. Just before she lit out for town she whispered to me that if I'd ride in later we could find us a justice of the peace and get hitched tonight."

"Look," Rowdy said sternly, "Kate knows blame well you made that crazy proposition just to get her to chase you into the badlands. She wouldn't really hold you to it."

"It ain't exactly that," Stumpy said. "Yuh see, Rowdy, a time or two in the past I've told you I'm gettin' too old for the sort of fool nonsense a feller runs into taggin' around with you. Comes a time when a gent has tuh seriously consider settlin' down. Now if you was to ride in with me and stand up as best man—"

Rowdy laid a gentle hand on his partner's shoulder. "I hate weddings worse than I hate good-byes," Rowdy said. "It would grieve me, pard, to stand there and see our partnership dissolved. Believe me, it would."

"Shucks, Rowdy, I only aim on gettin' married—not *buried!*"

"Just the same, it would bust me up to witness it."

"I was kinda countin' on yore support, Rowdy."

"Nervous, pard?"

"Wa-al, it makes a feller kind of shaky, just thinkin' of gettin' the knot tied."

In the moonlight Rowdy's choir boy face assumed a look of most cherubic innocence. Reaching into his boot top, he fished out the sheaf of currency and divided it into two even parts. One ward of bills he thrust into Stumpy's horny hand. "Here's half our money," Rowdy said. "You can't go before the J.P. with your knees knocking. What you need is a couple of bracers. When you hit town, go lap them up first thing."

"But I can't do that," Stumpy protested. "You know how Katharine feels about a drinking man!"

"Talk!" Rowdy scoffed. "The ladies like a real he-man who shows who's wearing the britches in the family. Here, you take this livery horse to town and swap him for my cayuse. I'll take your mount—an even trade. I'll be hitting the trail north toward the Missouri." He extended his hand. "And, Stumpy, if you should change your mind, I'll be riding slow."

Stumpy took the proffered hand. "I won't be changing my mind," he declared stoutly. "You look me up sometime, Rowdy—me and Katharine in our little love nest."

"Sure," Rowdy promised. "Don't forget those snifters."

And thus it was that Rowdy Dow rode alone from the Winged-H, picking his way through the moon-dappled badlands and riding without fear of each darkling shadow, for this land of weird rocks no longer held a menace. A few day's work had lifted a curse from this land, and in the thought of that was the real reward, abiding and satisfying. He came at long last to the trail that had fetched him and Stumpy toward Dryfooting, and he followed this trail northward until he looked down from rimrock upon the vast amphitheater where once he and his partner had watched hooded horsemen attacking a fancy stagecoach. This, Rowdy reflected, was like finishing out a circle, but he remembered friends left behind, and smiled.

He sat his saddle here for a long time, and then, his smile growing to a grin, he dismounted, hobbled Stumpy's horse and stripped the gear from the mount. Seated upon the saddle blanket, he smoked innumerable cigarettes and dozed a little; the moon disappeared beyond the western rim and the stars began to pale, and the first gray light was coloring the horizon when he heard the beat of hoofs.

"No wedding, Stumpy?" he asked as his partner rode up.

Stumpy unleased a vocabulary that made the rocks shudder. "She said she wouldn't marry me if I was the last man in the world," he added. "And I told her mighty plain that if I was the last man, she wouldn't have a chance. Confound such a woman, Rowdy, raising a ruckus just because a man had ten or twelve drinks!"

"She give you that shiner?"

Stumpy raised a hand to a swollen eye. "I collected this from the blacksmith," he said. "I never did rightly get it straight whether he give it me for something I did to him today, or whether he was sore because he come a-courtin' Katharine tonight and found me underfoot."

Rowdy began putting blanket and saddle on the horse, and when he mounted, Stumpy, who'd been mumbling to himself all the while, said suddenly, "Rowdy, you knew confounded well she'd call off the marriage if I stopped at the Tarantula fust!"

"Remember, I told you I was saving you from yourself," Rowdy said. "You'd have made a helluva husband!"

Stumpy began to laugh then, and Rowdy laughed with

him, and their laughter, real and clear and mighty loud, stirred up the echoes. And then they went riding stirrup to stirrup and shoulder to shoulder into the spreading dawn, never once looking back.